EXTRAORDINARY ACCLAIM FOR
THE COLD TRUTH

"Warning: don't pick up this book if you have only a few minutes to read . . . Jonathan Stone proves a master of delirious misdirection."
—*Tampa Tribune*

"Fast and furious, mazey and gothic, with a solution as chilling as an upstate New York winter. This is prime entertainment."
—Ian Rankin, Gold Dagger-winning author of
Dead Souls and *The Black Book*

"A spooky winner. This shiver delivers."
—Leslie Glass, bestselling author of *Judging Time*

"Jonathan Stone's THE COLD TRUTH is a strong debut. It's smart, fast and light on its feet. Stone has a gift for the whodunit, and he takes delight in spinning heads, playing with our emotions and our intellects, surprising us. I enjoyed THE COLD TRUTH—it's clever, bold, and a little nasty."
—T. Jefferson Parker, bestselling author of *Laguna Heat*

"The cold fact is that THE COLD TRUTH is a fantastic police procedural that introduces sub-genre fans to a host of wonderful characters."
—Harriet Klausner, Painted Rock Reviews

THE COLD TRUTH

Jonathan Stone

St. Martin's Paperbacks

THE COLD TRUTH

Copyright © 1999 by Jonathan Stone.

Excerpt from *The Heat of Lies* copyright © 2000 by Jonathan Stone.

Library of Congress Catalog Card Number: 98-43788

ISBN: 0-312-97143-5

Printed in the United States of America

St. Martin's Press hardcover edition / June 1999
St. Martin's Paperbacks edition / October 2000

St. Martin's Paperbacks are published by St. Martin's Press, 175 Fifth Avenue, New York, N.Y. 10010.

10 9 8 7 6 5 4 3 2 1

*This book was written in airplanes,
airport lounges, and hotel rooms,
but mostly on the 8:04 from Talmadge Hill;
I thank my fellow commuters for
their silence and forbearance . . .*

. . . and I thank Sue for the tone of our life

THE
COLD
TRUTH

Edwards stared down at the resumé wordlessly for what seemed an eternity. Julian listened to the metronomic click of the ceiling fan. She scanned the hastily labeled vertical brown file cases behind the Chief's ancient scarred chair, the chaotic paperwork piled on top of the files.

Every police-station cliché seemed to be covered, she thought. It looked like nothing had changed—or had even been moved—in decades.

Edwards looked up and stared straight at her for another eternity. The dinosaur chewed ruminatively, regarding her with limpid brown eyes empty of expression and yet infinitely capable of it, it seemed.

"I'd never have said yes to this whole Associate thing, which I was reluctant about anyway . . ." His voice rose, on the pain of remembering, it seemed, a whole chain of events. ". . . but you are, after all, the one I picked." He smiled grimly. "I rarely get fooled like this anymore."

He leaned back farther, settled the back of his head into some invisible, familiar notch in the ridged leather of the ancient chair. "Thirty years at it, see, you learn a thing or two." He studied her for a moment. She shifted uncomfortably. He waved his bear-paw hand vaguely in her direction.

"I know, for instance, the entire contents of

your shiny new briefcase there. Contains only a few more copies of this very impressive resumé"—he held it up again, shook it again—"and one yellow legal pad, because of the nasty habits you've picked up in this course here," pointing to Criminal Law on the resumé.

He looked up at her. "I know you got your hair cut just yesterday . . . the evenness of your bangs.

"And I know that the suit you're wearing, fresh-looking though it is, is an old one. Cuffs rolled under to make it fit." He cocked his head and now waved his big bear-paw more specifically at her suit.

Good Christ.

He studied her eyes with an almost optometric interest. "And I also know . . . well . . ." He stopped, waved his hand dismissively.

"What?" she said.

"Nothing." He shook his head.

"Go ahead."

He looked at her, still interested in her eyes. "I also know you masturbated this morning."

In that instant both saw it; both heard it: the arch of her tan body on the hotel bed. The familiar, final piercing cry.

But Julian didn't flinch.

"Eyes clear, no blood around the pupils," Edwards explained.

A lesson already, she thought.

"Relieving a little tension for the big interview," he said, with as much genuine understanding as sarcasm, she noticed.

"What makes you so sure I was alone?" she asked, unruffled.

He smiled bleakly. " 'Cause I know Canaanville."

"There's no there there," her classmates had warned. *"Fucking Arctic Circle. Sure, a legend. But Jesus. Ends of the earth. Time doesn't stand still? Hah! You'll see."*

Julian shifted, sat up. She looked at him. "This is a remarkable interview," she observed coolly.

"You're a remarkable woman," he said, waving the resumé by a corner again. "You deserve a remarkable interview."

He tilted up just slightly in the chair. "Shall we open the briefcase, see how I did?" he asked.

"No, you're correct," she said curtly.

"Entirely?"

She was silent.

He tilted back again, approaching horizontal. "But you see, for all my little tricks of thirty years' experience, I didn't know you were **a** woman."

He shook his head and smiled at her, and Julian detected something broadly in the neighborhood of affection.

"I could simply say no, the candidate was not right for us." He leaned back farther. She was surprised the ancient chair went back that far. It seemed a successful defiance of the laws of gravity.

And other laws? Did he defy them as easily?

"Hell, I could even say the candidate was a woman, and I don't want a woman in the job, and what are they gonna do, move up my retirement a few weeks? Which is upcoming, as I assume you were told.

"Tell you what I'll do, though. Give you a chance to prove an old dog wrong. A little test."

Julian tensed.

"Oh, now relax. Simple test. Much simpler test, I'm sure, than anything they had you doing here," he said, dangling the resumé once again, taunting. "See, all you've got to do in this test, is turn around."

Julian looked at him.

"Go ahead," he said genially, grandfatherly, "just turn around."

Entering Chief Edwards' office in her newly resurrected trim blue suit, quickly adjusting its hem, checking with a quick touch the clips in her coal-black hair, facing the famously irascible, and immense and backward and brilliant, Winston "Bear" Edwards for the first time, scanning the administrative chaos behind him while Edwards hunched over the resumé, Julian Palmer had never had the opportunity to notice the wall of Edwards' office behind her.

She looked at it now.

The head was far from the torso. Not so much severed as hacked at the neck into separateness. The torso no longer qualified as such: it was a spaghetti of flesh, a soup of organs, a jumble of bone. Sluices of blood and ligament flowed and seeped from the ribboned openings. The limbs bent in on themselves cartoonishly. The breasts were simply gone—in contrast to the head, cut cleanly off as if with surgical precision, leaving only rough, red-and-brown saucers where they had been. The eyes had been gouged; the nose and lips had been cut off, were missing, as if this were a manufactured doll, sent back now in pieces for impossible repairs. . . .

The layman would say bomb-blast victim. But Julian knew that the most powerful bomb blast would not have done this degree of damage.

Nor would some crazed animal.

Except one.

She knew immediately, with the lightning judgment that was a credit to and the pride of her forensics instructors, that this damage could only have been inflicted one way—by a human with a knife.

In numerous eight-by-ten and sixteen-by-twenty black-and-white photographs arrayed on the glass-partition wall of Chief Edwards' office, Julian Palmer took in, in a visual gulp, the most brutal murder she had ever seen.

She had seen, of course, a hundred throughout her schooling, and had studied them for evidence as dispassionately as if they were high-school science projects. She would even calculate later that in her training, she had probably seen more than Edwards, who, after all, didn't deal with them on a day-to-day basis. But this one still took the record for brutality.

Her intake of breath apparently went unnoticed by the Chief, behind her.

"Simms outside—lanky fella who showed you in—he was puking all morning when he saw these. Miz Palmer"—Winston Edwards said the Miz as sarcastically as possible—"you're hired. If you still want it, that is." The Great Chief Edwards extended his bear-paw hand. "Welcome."

And as for his earlier remarks on her preinterview activity, when both had accurately summoned up the familiar gymnastic . . . *arching, screaming* . . .

Well, mentioning it made it a moment of intimacy.

And the intimacy was, after all, simultaneous.

And you can't ask more of good partners than that.

TWO

In its infinitely suspect wisdom, the Great State of New York, with much fanfare, had instituted the Advanced Associates Internship Program just two years earlier. With equally dubious wisdom, it would eliminate the program just a year and a half later—a victim of shifting political breezes, the periodic cries of austerity, and legislators otherwise occupied and distracted.

The Advanced Associates Internship, in short, was one of those high-minded, well-intentioned, ill-conceived, and short-lived efforts that state legislators specialize in, which they initially tout highly and rally around; and then abandon, moving restlessly, reflexively, to the next problem, tackling it with some other high-minded program, to be similarly abandoned at some point hence.

The idea was to give police trainees a completely different police experience from the one they likely would know for the remainder of their professional lives: give the city trainee the vastly more generalized, subtler, and broader experience of rural police work; give the rural trainee the highly specialized, highly paced experience of city police work. (In truth, the program's main purpose was to provide big-city training to the rural recruit. Let him take new techniques back into the woods with him and, with any luck, begin to insinuate them into places still in the forensic dark.) New York was one of the few places that could confer the ultimate in both experiences—the thickest of the city, the farthest of upcountry—and that certainly was part of the program's initial fanfare and appeal.

But the program's origins, its politics, and its ultimate fate were far from Julian Palmer's mind, nowhere in her purview, as she read the brochure and quizzed the kindly, elderly half-informed Special Programs police counselor.

She was, in fact, thinking about snow.

She had never seen it. Not real snow. Oh sure, pictures of it. And of course, the cursory coating of the New York City streets around the Academy a few times, there for a moment, a blink, then plowed up and shoved aside and crusted with dirt by the time she got downstairs in the morning.

(New York's one utterly reliable efficiency, as far as she could tell.) And afternoon flurries that filled the sky with promise but, upon hitting the pavement, disappeared, turning into slush, melting into the ceaselessness of the city. So she had never really felt it, experienced it fully, looked out on a world of it. And while she knew that this would be a good thing for the resumé, and that this Winston Edwards was considered a major police talent, the snow was no small part of the appeal.

She smiled, amused to find herself thinking about it. Deep feet of it. A field of it. Fluffy, icy-cool, vivid at the edge of her imagination, and now, in every sense, within her grasp. Because her request (you could request a specific region—that was part of the bait) could put her squarely in it.

The Snow Belt, they called it. A narrow geographic band from east of the Great Lakes at the Canadian border to just north of Pittsburgh. A surprisingly narrow geographical swath where geothermal and topographical conditions conspired to produce an inordinate amount of the stuff.

Colder places got less. Higher elevations got less. The Snow Belt got hammered, blanketed in white silence, then blanketed and blanketed again.

There was something about that white blanket that captivated her. . . .

It seemed like a way of forgetting. A way of

softly covering everything up. Of starting anew. A way she hadn't tried. And though she only half admitted it to herself, only half recognized it, that was what fascinated her about snow most of all.

What it could bury. What it could cover. What it could silence. What it could do, a season in the cleansing cold.

And then—in the next instant—she was thinking about the program, its possibilities. Ever-practical, she had given the snow its thought, its due, and moved on to think about what she needed to. Focused. Sharp. Trained.

She couldn't know, of course, that what would happen to her up there in the snow would hasten the end of the Advanced Associates Internship Program; would account for at least one angry speech on the legislature floor; would contribute powerfully to the sour taste in the legislature's mouth . . .

For now, it was that snow, the vision of it, alluring, beckoning, wondrous, cool, that compelled her to take pen in hand in the tiny office of the Special Programs counselor, and swiftly, eagerly, competently, fill out the application.

THREE

A closer inspection of the Canaanville station house the following morning revealed that it was not quite the archaic movie set it had first appeared. Beneath an assortment of files there was a fax machine. Beneath an inexplicable collection of neatly folded plastic bags there was even a personal computer. It was as if the patina of ceiling fans and dust and wooden chairs hid the workings of a reasonably efficient office of criminal investigation.

Not unlike the exterior of its gruff leader, Julian reflected.

"So how'd you like the pictures?" Julian heard suddenly behind her, and she spun around, startled, and instinctively, to find Simms, mildly leering, unmildly gap-toothed, and standing inappropriately close beside her, Julian noticed, like an upcountry in-bred idiot, or, come to think of it, a petty bureaucrat now in the safe employ of New York State.

Julian shrugged noncommittally.

"That's how he's always done it," Simms said, fairly glowing with pride over his superior and encyclopedic knowledge of the famous ways of the Chief. "Puts 'em up on wall, stares at 'em, broods and sulks and stares 'em down some more, and then one day, lo and behold, he's got the solution. Pretty bizarre, huh?"

Julian saw that Simms' last sentence was not merely rhetorical. He was actually waiting for a reply. And in an instant she could tell years' worth of office politics: that Simms and the others found the Chief and his methods exceedingly strange, and that they wanted Julian to find him strange also. Simms, she suddenly knew, was the emissary. Where did she stand?

She didn't want to offend them, but she didn't want them to place her in the wrong camp.

So she smiled. She smiled broadly, affectionately, winningly, a smile she'd called on plenty.

I know what you mean, that smile said.

You poor slobs don't know a police talent when you see one, the smile said.

The choice was theirs.

* * *

"What you are looking at, *Miz* Julian Palmer," said Chief Edwards, gesturing to the brutal pictures again, "is another matter—more serious than that of your gender—in which, it would seem, my thirty years' experience are failing me." He slurped the coffee as if it were life itself, and then, after having gulped half a cup, paused to smell it, as if checking it well after the fact for acceptability— or poison—before continuing. "Let me give you *her* resumé. A bit less impressive perhaps, and a whole lot briefer, than yours. Sarah Langley. Twenty-one. Waitress. Single. Lived alone on Southside."

Which Julian knew already, from her quick self-tour around the town the night before. Every older city, small or large, had its blighted section, it seemed, its cancerous cluster that police officers, like crude physicians, sought to contain, in vague worry over a rampant spreading. In a city like Canaanville, that was itself blighted, its "poorer" section was poorer than most.

"All wounds inflicted with an eight-inch knife, and hands, and brute strength," the Chief said in an unnecessarily declamatory way, and then lowered his voice a respectful half-step to add, "forty-four knife wounds, to be exact. Knife not found. Local girl. No clues. By which I mean, none. Unsolved one month exactly as of this morning."

Chief Edwards paused. "Which is two weeks longer than any investigation in this office has remained unsolved." He said it suddenly, Julian noticed, as if to fully shoulder the pain of it, as if to take on the full weight of its responsibility.

Another kind of "bear," it occurred to her. As in: *to bear; the bearer.*

Julian watched Edwards walk in front of the pictures. He looked down at his feet, examined his shoes, as if searching closely for the essential clue there in the faded overworked leather or the frayed laces; looked suddenly up at the photographs, at one or the other, for a long moment; then down at his shoes; then walked again. He paused, then looked more generally at a picture here, a picture there, like a half-interested tourist in a gruesomely hip art gallery. He then went back to his desk and sat as heavily and laboriously as, Julian would shortly learn, he always sat.

"She weren't no Phi Beta Kappa," he said over his bifocals, with what Julian now knew was a mocking misuse of the language only for effect, "and she weren't no belle of the ball. But let me tell you this, Miz Palmer. This was a young woman, with her own little dreams, which probably didn't extend much beyond this little town's boundaries and her own little life, which will now sure as shit *not* extend beyond them. And while we work, Miss Big City"—an unmistakable, unsuppressible hint of hostility—"do not think for a moment that we are looking for the killer of the girl in those pictures."

What?

"We are not looking for the killer of the girl in those pictures," Edwards asserted again to her puzzled expression.

Edwards opened his desk drawer, took out what was clearly a high-school yearbook portrait of an appealing, blond somehow so eager, farm-raised country girl in her ill-fitting but best dress, and held it for Julian to see. "We are looking for *this* girl's killer." He turned the picture so they could both see it, so they could contemplate it together. "Sarah Langley. A real girl. A person. A life."

Edwards continued looking at the picture a moment more. "Her parents showed it to me." He squinted at it, glanced up at Julian. "I asked if I could keep it." Edwards reached laboriously into his back pocket, took out his wallet, unfolded it, and slipped the girl's picture into the wallet's already straining creases. He looked at Julian grimly. "You can imagine what a pleasant conversation that was.

"Thirty years, I've never had one unsolved in

this jurisdiction." He smiled. "So your timing's pretty interesting."

He leaned back again, studied her a moment. "Now, I don't know all that much 'bout what they teach you at that Academy of yours, though I got some ideas. . . ."

"You're just a 'country boy,' " she said sardonically.

"Yeah, somethin' like that. Point is, I'm gonna try out a little phrase on you here, and I'll tell you right now, I'm only sayin' it to watch your reaction. 'Cause I got a theory about how you're gonna react, and how your reaction's gonna change real soon. Plus, I don't want you hearin' this phrase as proof positive that you're way the hell up here in the woods."

She grew impatient. "What's the phrase?"

Edwards studied her. "The Perfect Crime."

"The Perfect Crime," she repeated, managing to suppress her reaction to the mere hint of a smile.

The dinosaur rises again, she thought. *It's a movie. I'm in a movie.*

Edwards, fortunately, smiled too. "Stupid phrase, I know. But over the years of this, you see the mistakes a criminal makes. The patterns of them. And in certain cases, the absence of pattern. You say, 'Gee, if he'd've only . . .' and, 'Gee, if he'd only thought to . . .' So you start to wonder whether—to see how—there could be a Perfect Crime."

He looked out the big dirty window to the elaborate cornice of the Rhine Brothers Hardware building across the street—now Ace Hardware, Julian had noticed, the shiny metal corporate-affiliation sign much more strident and clean compared to the faded, barely discernible lettering of Rhine Brothers. The Rhine Brothers cornice was the only thing visible from the Chief's back-leaning angle, Julian saw, apart from gray, empty November sky. "This will seem like an awful arrogant thing to say, but people around here ain't generally all that bright," the Chief said, "although please don't repeat that opinion to any of them. They're bright enough, at least, to know that ain't too flattering." He smiled. "And I've long considered myself about the brightest, which believe me, says more about the people around here than about me. But I catch myself thinking every so often that we are finally looking at a perfect one."

"No such thing," Julian asserted. It was the first professional opinion ventured in Edwards' presence.

"Is that the official Academy position?"

As if she had no opinion of her own.

"The Academy didn't have an official position," she retorted. "That's just my gut feeling about it. Believe it or not, I do have instincts."

He smiled. "Glad to hear that. Quite glad. We're gonna do all right." His smile, she noticed, was different now—different from his previous smiles. This one seemed somehow . . . well, what? Sincere?

FOUR

Having parked his Impala in his driveway, trudged up the manicured walk and up the porch steps of his immaculate gingerbread Victorian home, having hung up his coat on its accustomed Shaker peg, relieved himself laboriously in the powder-blue guest toilet, and washed his hands thoroughly, Chief Edwards now sat down to dinner in the tiny dining room with its pretentious frieze of Greek figurines, wondering how he would explain to his wife—his wife of a corpulence and rotundity that daily threatened to match his own—the presence of this new, polished, disconcertingly attractive assistant.

Perhaps his wife would not believe he had been so fooled by the gender of the name. He could hardly believe it himself. He was not relishing the task of telling her, but it had to be done. Canaanville had the soul of a small town. And news, he knew, made it even smaller.

To compound matters, she served him his favorite: a big porterhouse steak, done black-and-blue, with a significant hill of beans, and opposite on the plate—like an equally formidable opponent in the other corner of the ring—a not-to-be-outdone mound of black-eyed peas.

"Well . . ." He began cautiously, and wondered why, after all these years, with all these people in his command and the obvious and often over-weaning respect accorded him, he still cowered at this woman. "We, uh . . ." he said, "we've got that new assistant. Started today."

"Oh, really? How's that working out?" The Missus worked her steak and beans with all the expertise and aggression of her husband, who found himself for the moment not all that hungry.

"Going to be fine. . . ." He'd better get to it or he really would be in trouble.

"Nice young man?" she asked, abstractly chewing, bovine accompaniment. . . .

"Well, no. . . ."

Mrs. Edwards looked up slowly, expectantly, awaiting further explanation.

Now or never.

"Turned out to be a woman."

Her look, over her own bifocals, was a mirror

of his own. Sometimes he even saw his own bifocals reflected in hers.

"Her damn name fooled me."

She looked at him, smiled, and dug into her food with new gusto. "Nice young woman?"

"Mm-hmm." It was all he could manage.

"Where's she living?" she asked, with new concern in her voice.

"Only place she can, time being. The Ramada."

"That's no place for a young woman to be staying. How long'll she be here?"

"Program lasts couple a months."

He hadn't yet gotten to the subject of the woman's appearance, but Edwards had a sudden sinking feeling. He knew where this was heading.

They had a barn about two hundred yards down a path from the main house, with a nicely furnished apartment, and over the years they had idly threatened to rent it out, but there was never really the need, financially, nor the inclination. It had come in handy when the kids had been noisy teens, but they were long gone now. He hadn't thought about it, until this moment.

The porterhouse—his favorite dish, under normal circumstances—looked worse and worse. If he wanted to take a bite of the steak, he would have to bite the bullet.

He debated dropping into the conversation casually the woman's beauty, but he decided that would be even worse.

He pushed his plate away.

"Estelle. . . ."

"Yes?" She looked up again with her simple, honest regard.

So just say it.

"Estelle, the woman is quite pretty."

Pretty, good Christ. The girl was an assault. Tongues lolled, eyes lingered, the deadly-dull second floor of the station house had been whip-cracked alive by lust. A hormonal jolt. Hilarious, all that longing, if it weren't so indescribably serious, too. It was a crude joke, wheeling her into cold November on them; her tailored trim blue suit seemed only to say that its contents couldn't be contained in it.

Likewise her black hair—deep, remarkable, lustrous—pinned up severely, yet so obviously luxuriant, straining at the hairclips, strands and locks loosening impatiently even in the course of the short interview. Framing an oval face—smooth and pale, clear-eyed and healthy—the canopy-bed or backseat genetic accomplishment, Edwards thought cynically, of some down-home beauty and handsome rogue. But more than that—the way those smooth pale features somehow came to a point; how they organized, aligned with purpose and mission, with focus and alertness, at the end of her nose; creating an impression of intensity, the added beauty of intensity.

Genes, boy. Genes that did that. That found their mark.

Estelle looked at him. "Pretty. So?"

"Well . . . nothing, I guess . . . just so's you know, 'case you hear anything."

"And what would I hear?"

He shrugged. "Nothin'. But it's a small town."

"I don't know that?"

He smiled. "We both know that."

And that was that. Which showed how he could still be fooled, not just by a name on a resumé, but by his own wife of thirty years.

They ate in their accustomed silence.

"Anything on the murder?"

He looked up suddenly at her.

He felt a kind of crackle, a sizzle, ignite his brain. A blast of anger coursed through his body. *Why does she do that? Why?*

Their eyes locked.

He put down his fork. Turned it idly on the table.

"No, nothing on the murder," he managed to say evenly.

"Investigation's gotten no closer?"

"Investigation's gotten no closer."

"So nobody's gotten any—"

"Jesus, Estelle." He felt the familiar rage pulse in him. "*Please*. Let's not discuss it."

"I shouldn't of brought it up," she said after a pause.

They looked silently at each other.

"I won't bring it up again," she said.

And once the silence had hung over them long enough to inflict all the agony a silence can, he looked around the dining room of his immaculate Victorian home, at the pretentious Greek frieze, at the delectable porterhouse and twin mountains of beans and not-to-be-outdone black-eyed peas, across at his wife of thirty years, whose corpulence and rotundity daily threatened to match his own, and gradually, with the satisfying thought that everything, to all outward observance, still appeared as would be expected, he relaxed a little again, and ventured another bite.

And in silence, a heavy silence—a heavier silence than most will ever know—Winston and Estelle Edwards continued their dinner.

FIVE

The next morning, Julian Palmer was put on payroll, assigned her own little section of beat-up linoleum floor outside Edwards' office, and listened to Chief Edwards carefully list her duties with a huge finger held aloft to visually accompany and accentuate each one.

The duties were centered, for the moment, at a big ancient metal desk, a gift of the downsizing of the school district, as Julian discovered when she cleaned children's tests from 1958 out of its drawers.

The duties also included answering the phone, opening the Chief's mail—and Julian was getting the sense that Edwards, not surprisingly, was of the start-at-the-bottom school of criminology.

She also sensed that Chief Edwards didn't quite know what to do with her, so he had concocted this full schedule of duties as if to keep her from the realization.

She didn't mind. It was a way to get settled, get to know the area, the people, the Chief's routine.

Just so long as he didn't intend this to shut her out of the real work.

"Now in this station house we have a sign-in policy. Everybody comes in through the entrance—and I mean *everybody* not on the payroll of this police department—signs the logbook. Messengers, water delivery, insurance salesman, prostitutes, *everybody* signs in. So we got a record—no theft, no problems, no second-guessing," he said sternly. "Iron rule that's helped us out here more than once, when evidence has suddenly disappeared, et cetera."

What was this, first grade? Or, on the other hand, was she aboard a tight ship?

Underneath it all, the place definitely wasn't as dusty as it first appeared.

Throughout the morning, she watched Edwards pace on the other side of the glass partition, brood and sulk in front of the photographs, just as Simms had promised, while she answered phone calls.

The calls to Chief Edwards were—as she knew all police work was—enormously routine. Lawyers needing to check testimony and the Chief's availability to testify. City and county officials and civil servants of variously ascertainable function, requesting duplicates and triplicates of paperwork, clarifications. Parole officers wishing to discuss reports. It was a crushing weight of paperwork. Osmium, according to the periodic table, was the heaviest substance known to man. But Julian knew better. She knew it was paper.

"I suppose a welcome lunch is in order," said Edwards to Julian at noontime.

In moments, they were at the counter of Rhine Brothers Hardware, where Edwards was not even offered a menu, but where instead a heaping sandwich was put in front of him so quickly that he hardly had to look for it before reaching for a bite.

Julian, however, received a printed menu with a courtly flourish from the old counterman; and cook, counterman, and cashier seemed to hover with as much curiosity about what she would order, it seemed, as about her.

Careful not to ask for a salad and fulfill any clichés or satisfy Edwards' detecting skills (better to sabotage them a bit), she went with a tuna melt and a cola—as noncommittal and unrevealing a lunch as possible, from the narrow confines of Rhine Brothers' selections.

"I hardly have to mention, I guess, that I've eaten lunch here almost every day for thirty years. I usually take it with the morning paper, but today, obviously, is a special occasion. Hope that tuna's okay."

She took a huge bite in answer.

"How's the Ramada?" he asked.

"It's a Ramada," she managed, when she finally swallowed.

"Never actually stayed there, of course. But I've been in there." He looked up suddenly. "Investigating, of course."

Julian smiled. "I understand."

He looked relieved. "Rooms don't seem that bad. Clean."

This was painful, thought Julian. Why had he suggested lunch? Presumably because he thought he should. Because it was the appropriate thing to do. She wondered if that was the only reason.

He looked at her.

Some girl.

The words drifted into Winston Edwards' mind freely, dreamily, abstractly, then focused sharp, tense, into a thought:

That that's all that was left now of the girl in the photographs, wasn't it?

Some girl.

*   *   *

The call came early that afternoon.

"Chief Edwards' office, can I help you?" She had begun a cheerful, singsongy response that she hated hearing herself make. She hoped she wouldn't be at this desk forever.

"Is he there?" The voice was raspy, male, strangely measured and articulate.

"Who may I say is calling, please?" She was learning the secretarial tricks quickly: not saying he was in, but not saying he wasn't.

"Is Chief Edwards there?" The raspy voice asked the question again so evenly, it was as if he had never asked it it the first time. And as if her response—and she—did not exist.

Two could play that game. "Who may I say is calling, please?"

"My name is Wayne Hill, and I think I can help him on the Langley case."

Julian Palmer sat up in the chair.

She had, of course, already fielded her share of calls on the murder. Breathless. Hysterical. Portentous. Ominous. In short, cranks. At Edwards' instructions, she had assigned the perfunctory interviews to Simms, fully aware that nothing would come of them.

But this voice, first of all, had given a name

and, by its calm and intelligent tone, established authority.

Could be something.

Her back straightened to attention. She glanced in at the Chief through the glass partition, waved her hands, trying to get his attention.

He was reading something at his desk and didn't look up.

Her training told her how to handle a call like this, but she didn't know whether Edwards would agree with that training.

"Mr. Hill, I'm Julian Palmer, Chief Edwards' assistant. Can I help you?"

She heard the man breathe impatiently.

She waved frantically now for Chief Edwards and, not knowing what else to do, balled up the report uppermost in her desk's pile, and threw it hard against the partition.

That got him. He looked up, annoyed.

She pointed nervously to the phone.

Huge Edwards was through the partition door and standing next to her in a blink. Expressionless, alert.

She felt relief, she noticed, and continued. "May I tell Chief Edwards the nature of your assistance?"

"Yes. I'm a psychic."

She covered the mouthpiece, and looked up.

Edwards waited, breath bated.

She tried to utter it, but the words caught in her throat.

"Well?!"

Oh brother, she thought.

"Come on!"

She took a breath. "He's a psychic," she muttered, half swallowing it, wholly hoping to, and screwing up her mouth in shame.

"What?!"

She blinked. Then realized he hadn't heard her. She was forced to say it again, louder, clearer. "A psychic."

Winston Edwards rolled his eyes, and hulked and sulked, a wounded bear, back toward his office.

He turned back to her at his office door, glowering, as if to remind her of the lesson.

Then he snorted a laugh.

Thank God.

But now, what to do with Wayne Hill, Psychic? She dangled the receiver, and looked at Edwards questioningly. Edwards shrugged. "We'll get back to him." And he shut the partition door.

Of course, police departments did employ psychics. It was one of criminology's dirty little standing secrets. No police department, trying to present a modern face to its taxpayer base, was too eager to admit that it paid a psychic. And police detectives, constitutionally skeptical, cringed when the association occurred. But despite all this, Julian had learned at the Academy, a surprising number of police departments did use them. Particularly in places steeped in past methods. Places unshaken in their ways of doing things, and unexamined by the wider world. Places like Canaanville. Although Julian had immediately assumed that the great Winston Edwards did not use psychics; and she had apparently assumed right.

SIX

The easy thing would be to dismiss the idea as some ridiculous backwater nineteen-thirties kind of thing . . ." Chief Edwards said, leaning back in his hair expansively. "Something to go with these ceiling fans and metal files."

He leaned forward purposefully. "But let's look at the facts. This investigation has gone nowhere in over a month. *Over* a month. Nothing. Zip. So how would it look," he continued, "if I didn't chase down every possibility? Look down every blind alley. Particularly on what could be my swan song. I've always prided myself on following up everything. Being dogged.

"I can't let it be said I didn't try everything. That I didn't give it my damnedest. And if I didn't try this psychic, they'd have a right to say that.

"I mean, what would *you* say if I didn't pursue

every avenue? You wouldn't be too impressed, either. So I risk a few guffaws. So what?

"And, strictly speaking, it would be impeding an investigation—potentially withholding evidence—not to at least try, wouldn't it?"

He leaned back, twirled a pencil, cocked his head, and continued. "You will, I'm sure, find this horrifying," said Edwards, "you may find this even more horrifying than the pictures on the wall behind you, but believe it or not, I have worked with psychics before."

Julian looked at him evenly, trying now not to approve or disapprove or judge in any way. But she was astonished, and still absorbing the prospect—the foregone conclusion—of a new, peculiar partner in the investigation.

"And have you ever had any luck with any of these guys?"

"Well . . ." He smiled slowly. "No. Not in the least."

"Then, why now?" she said, palms open.

He looked at her, suddenly serious. "I don't know what they teach you at that Academy, but I do know we have a kind of Golden Rule for police work. The short course. Rule is: Whatever works."

"But you just said psychics had been of no use to you."

He smiled. "I've been holding out a little on

you, Miz Palmer. I did a little investigating last night. Mr. Wayne Hill, Psychic, is—as far as these things go, anyway—the real thing. He's got, it turns out, a Reputation, with a big *R*. I've got a lot of friends in this state, and I called around, and an old pal of mine, Chief Richards, over in Northward, turns out, has worked with Wayne Hill on two big murder cases further upstate, one of which, he claims, Mr. Hill essentially solved. Though on the next case, he says, they got nowhere, still unsolved, matter of fact. That was the last Richards had heard of him, till now."

He waited for a reaction, but Julian was simply listening.

"Says he's a strange bird, but hell, that's certainly par for the course. So put in a call to Mr. Hill, if you would, and let's see him here sometime tomorrow, if that's possible."

He looked at her with a wry smile as she rose to leave. "And Miz Palmer . . ." he said.

"Yes?"

He looked at her affectionately. "Let us try, during our interview with Mr. Hill, to maintain a sense of decorum."

"Meaning?"

"Meaning I won't laugh if you don't." He leaned back over his paperwork, as Julian rose from the chair.

She felt a funny, freeing, inexplicable lightness in the room. Carried on the tone of a mild, harmless flirtatiousness, she heard her own words escape her. "Why do you need a psychic? You already knew everything about my suit and my briefcase and . . ." She paused, but somehow felt comfortable enough to say it. ". . . my morning?"

He looked up at her one more time. "It's true, I am a little psychic myself," he said with a smile. "I can tell you, for instance, what's no longer in your briefcase."

He was right. She'd finally taken the resumés out.

Julian dialed the number Hill had left her. She let it ring almost a dozen times, and just as she was about to hang up—

"H'lo?" slurred a male voice. Clearly not the man she had spoken to before.

"Is Wayne Hill there, please?"

"Who?" said the voice loudly, and she could tell now the man was drunk.

"Wayne Hill."

"Who's that?" said the slurred voice accusingly.

"Wayne Hill. He left this number . . . I'm sorry, I must have dialed—"

"Wayne Hill!" the man suddenly yelled out at the other end.

There was a clicking and loud banging over the receiver, and the raspy and even and educated voice returned.

"Yes, this is Wayne Hill."

"Mr. Hill, Julian Palmer, Chief Edwards' assistant. The Chief would be pleased to see you tomorrow afternoon."

"Ah, Miss Palmer. Forgive my current living arrangements. And thank you for getting back to me. I'm quite pleased. Very good." And through the raspy but even and professional voice, Julian could hear that the man was indeed pleased, even thankful. And in short order, after an exchange of pleasantries (to prove to her he was only human, Julian would reflect later), and after a brief coordination of scheduling and travel arrangements, Wayne Hill concluded the conversation with what might otherwise have been a perfectly reasonable request, or one that at least might be reasonably expected of a psychic. Yet when Julian heard it, her stomach sank, for she was doomed to be the messenger.

"Chief Edwards?"

"Yes?" said Edwards cheerfully, looking up from his desk.

"He asked . . ." She stalled. There was something in her, she discovered in that moment, that did not want to disappoint him.

"Yes?"

"He asked for all crime photographs on display to be gathered in an envelope, given to someone who has no knowledge of the contents . . ."

"That's how he's always done it. Puts 'em up on his wall . . .," Simms had said.

She could hear Edwards breathe . . . heavier.

Edwards looked at the wall of photos and then blankly back at her. "You do it," he said, and abruptly stood up and left his office.

Julian watched the door close behind him with just enough force to mark his displeasure. In a moment, she began to remove the gruesome photographs.

With her slowly developing instincts, she had the feeling Edwards would regret his decision to contact Wayne Hill.

SEVEN

Wayne Hill—jet-black hair combed back, eyebrows that almost met—was dressed simply and unremarkably in corduroy pants and a cardigan sweater, and his unremarkable overall appearance made his hands seem all the more unusual.

They were large, both held in a painful-looking, arthritic half-clutch, and the left hand was missing its last finger.

Missing fingers were fairly common around Canaanville, Julian had already observed—the all-too-frequent results of chain-saw and farm-machinery accidents—but Mr. Hill, pallid, fragile-looking, didn't look like he'd ever been close to a farm.

Wayne Hill sat in the chair where Julian Palmer had been interviewed and where she usually sat in her dealings with the Chief, and Hill's being

seated there for some reason made her vaguely uncomfortable.

So what happens now? wondered Julian. *Falling into a trance, swooning, speaking in tongues?*

"Coffee, Mr. Hill?" offered Edwards. Before
this, Julian hadn't once seen Edwards offer anything to or behave solicitously toward anyone in
this office, his domain.

"No, thank you," said that raspy voice, quiet,
unassuming, with a short, curt, diffident smile.

"Appreciate your coming down here on short
notice like this."

Hill waved off the sentiment as unnecessary.
He behaved, in the cursory and largely social moments at the opening of the interview, much like
an expert witness. If this was his natural professionalism, then there was something about him Julian instinctively liked.

"Now, as you can well imagine, we've been
checking you out. Some excellent credentials," said
Edwards. "Like Julian here, a resumé very impressive for your own chosen field."

"It chose me," Wayne Hill said curtly.

Edwards looked up, and Julian immediately
saw the look of bemusement on Edwards' face.
She sensed all of a sudden that Edwards had been
lying in wait, waiting for an opening, and now he
had one. "So what's wrong with that? You've got

a terrific occupation, way I see it. Flexible hours. Work when you want." Eyebrows raised high, creasing his forehead magnificently, Edwards doodled with a pen with surprising delicacy. "The chance to be *very* creative."

"Very funny," said Wayne Hill, unamused.

"Hey, people would kill for your job," Edwards went on, affecting good nature, making his hostility all the more apparent.

But Hill proved to be up to Edwards' banter. "Job's being phased out, if you hadn't noticed."

"Like blacksmiths," said Edwards.

"Like barrel coopers," said Hill.

"Ever noticed most psychics are women?" observed Edwards. "Why is that, do you think?"

Hill was silent.

"Kind of a feminine profession?"

Hill held his silence.

"And what's with the hand?" asked Edwards, just like that.

"It's missing a finger," said Wayne Hill archly.

"The Pike Twin murders," Edwards went on, unruffled, unpausing, as if unaware of his bluntness, "they say you solved those outright. And invaluable assistance, I'm told, *invaluable* assistance, on the so-called Church Bell homicide. But then you just dropped out of sight, for"—Edwards checked his notes—"well over a year now. What can you tell us about that?" Edwards asked, watching Hill carefully.

Wayne Hill shrugged noncommittally. "There's not much to tell, really. I was assisting on a case upstate, but I was feeling . . ." He shifted in his chair, as if from an itch, and seemed to focus elsewhere for a moment. And then, in the next moment, seemed to remember where he was. ". . . well, nothing." He shrugged again, and was silent.

"Huh!" said Edwards, as if as baffled by it as Hill. Boy, Edwards was good, thought Julian. Because it left an opening, a silence like a vacuum, which Hill might feel compelled to fill. But he did not. He sat waiting.

"And now?"

"I suddenly had a feeling," said Hill. "It was in the papers, and I just suddenly had a feeling."

He sounded as if he would go further. He leaned forward.

Edwards paused, waiting.

But Hill added no more.

Edwards continued. "According to my notes here, during this period when you've been feeling . . . uh, 'nothing,' as you say, you've been fairly regular with—in fact, pretty much living in—the Mental Health Unit of Zimmern Upstate Hospital, isn't that correct?"

Julian managed not to react, but she wished the Chief had briefed her beforehand.

"That's correct," Wayne Hill affirmed.

"And what was that all about?"

"What was that all about?" Nice and wide-open, Julian noticed again. *Let him tell you whatever he wants.* Julian had to admit, she was learning a thing or two.

"Well," said Hill, "I'd lost this . . . this whatever it is. I was trying to figure out what to do. I was . . . well, confused."

Again there was a silence.

Again Hill was going no further. "Any other questions, Chief Edwards?"

As if to say, *My life is an open book,* thought Julian. As if to say, *I have nothing to hide. I'm the genuine article, now let's get down to business.*

Yet not expanding, not telling them any more than they needed to know.

Edwards shrugged, looked over his notes. "No, not really. You could just confirm that . . . uh, according to my notes and conversation, says here you like a supply of—this right?—fresh cranberries kept in stock when you're on a case. And you won't allow your picture to be taken."

"Correct," Hill said officiously, not elaborating.

"Steals your soul, does it?"

"Something like that."

It was as if by some code psychics and detectives expected and agreed not to like one another, Julian thought, because Edwards and Hill simply went right on.

"Not a terribly long list of quirks, for someone in your profession," conceded Edwards with a smile. "Well, okay then," he said. "Pictures, per your instructions, are in a large manila envelope in one of the outer offices. . . ."

Edwards said this quite cheerfully. A little joke for Julian's benefit, she knew, considering how Edwards had, with silent but very apparent fury, stormed out of his own office earlier when Julian reluctantly relayed Hill's request.

"All of the pictures? That's important."

"Yes. All of them, as you asked. Shall we bring them in?"

"Yes, please. If whoever has been keeping the photographs could carry them in . . ."

Edwards motioned to Julian to bring in the temporary receptionist.

Julian escorted in an elderly woman holding the envelope under her arm, who looked quizzically at all of them.

"Hand it to him," Julian instructed gently, pointing to Hill.

The woman looked at the envelope suspiciously—the envelope Julian wouldn't carry for herself. The woman passed it halfway to Hill, but abruptly stopped. "What's in here, anyway?" she asked cautiously.

"Nothing," said Julian.

" 'Nothing'?" mocked the woman.

"Just photographs," said Julian. "Please."

Bewildered, the woman put the envelope into Hill's strange hands, recoiled slightly on seeing the missing finger, regarded them all as conspiratorially insane, and left.

Oddly, for the elaborate presentation he had insisted upon, Wayne Hill opened the envelope quickly and unceremoniously and riffled through the photos as if they were junk mail.

"Sarah Langley—," began Winston Edwards.

"I know," said Wayne Hill, cutting Edwards off.

But her name had been in the newspapers, Julian noted.

Edwards tried to begin again. "As you can see, stab wounds—"

"Forty-six," said Hill.

Edwards looked startled.

Julian was startled. *That* hadn't been in the papers. Edwards had said forty-four. How could he so quickly . . . ?

"Forty-six," Hill asserted. He studied the pictures now, more slowly, individually, and in his raspy voice she heard him begin to mutter to himself, "Two times twenty-three—twice a prime—as in suspect, huh? . . ." He looked up at them, and Julian was further startled by how Wayne Hill's eyes seemed, for that instant, inexplicably changed. "Forty-six—number of human chromosomes—number that symbolizes life, mmm? . . ." And then he abandoned them, descended into a mild mutter and hum—indecipherable, barely audible, yet utterly ordinary, like a clerk adding columns or a weary manager tallying up at closing time: "Prime . . . The prime of life—as in cut down in the . . . cut down . . ." Abstracted, raspy-voiced, throaty—all the while studying the pictures. Julian could make out only some of the phrases. He emitted a short low chuckle as a strange final punctuation, turned, looked up at both of them.

Julian didn't know what she had expected, exactly. But—granting the benefit of the doubt for the moment to the whole notion of psychic ability—she did expect that if those photographs could evoke the reactions they did in regular police investigators, they must do something remarkable in the highly attuned minds and sensitivities of psychic sensation. Here he had said forty-six wounds almost immediately. But apart from that, Wayne

Hill seemed to be registering no reaction. He simply studied the photographs almost disinterestedly, cycling through them quickly again now, like snapshots, looking almost as an afterthought.

Then he glanced down at his hands, those stiff, misshapen hands, as if to see whether he needed to trim his nails.

"White shoes," he said, barely audibly, as if in passing.

"What's that?"

"I see white shoes."

White shoes?

There were no shoes in the photographs.

Edwards looked blankly at him. "Anything else?"

Hill looked at his hands, then looked up and shook his head. "No." He smiled. "Sorry."

"You think you could make yourself available, to, uh, come see us again tomorrow?"

"You're putting me up?" Hill asked tentatively.

Edwards nodded.

"Thank you," said Hill, truly graciously, it seemed to Julian. And then he drew himself up out of his habitual crouch, and surprised them by making, in his raspy, straining voice, a little speech.

"I know how hard it is for police, with their professional, necessary skepticism, to accept the idea of a spiritual constellation. But I really think

I can help on this. I really did sense something, and it's the first time in a long time. Please bear with me. I honestly think I can help."

It was almost a plea—not the arrogant, haughty assistance that Julian had presumed for a psychic. He directed his little speech at her, Julian noticed, before turning part of it toward the Chief—only to be appropriate, it seemed to her.

Then again, he might just be cleverly begging for his meal ticket.

"So where will I be staying?" asked Hill.

"Only place you can," Edwards said. "The Ramada," turning with a playful grin toward Julian.

Oh, wonderful.

"So what is this with white shoes?" Julian asked Edwards. "There were no shoes in the photographs. I assume none were found . . ."

Edwards was settling back in the ancient chair.

"And the forty-six wounds?" she asked. "What was that? The newspapers said forty-four. *You* said forty-four."

"Body in a state like that, you can't be sure how many wounds there are, exactly," Edwards said. "As anyone involved with police work would know. And as Mr. Hill, after his own close involvement with police work, would certainly know."

"Then he's a fake?" asked Julian.

"Could be," said Chief Edwards. "But in any case, not quite the circus barker you were expecting, I'll wager."

"But that kind of mild disinterest, and then the sudden quiet intensity. It could be the most sophisticated circus act in the world," Julian said.

"He didn't prove he knew anything," said Edwards. "And he didn't prove he didn't. Jury's still out. So I'm putting him up." He was pensive.

"So what about those white shoes?"

"Well," said Edwards, rising, squinting out the window to Rhine Brothers across the street, "the victim's shoes were black."

At four A.M., in the Victorian-wallpapered bedroom of his Victorian home, absurdly delicate for the girth and heft and manner of its two inhabitants, Edwards awoke with a start, breathing heavily; sat suddenly upright with the long-gone vigor of the younger, leaner man within him.

He had been dreaming about the dead girl. Sarah Langley.

His pulse pounded. His heart rapped angrily at his chest.

The dreaming always happened on murder cases. So there was nothing unusual about that.

With all the brooding about them, obsessing about them, you couldn't help but dream about them.

It had happened on all his murder cases that he could think of. So why shouldn't it happen on this one? That was perfectly normal, wasn't it? Why should this one be any different?

He looked next to him. Estelle slumbered like a bear. She'd gotten used to this sudden awakening of his over the years. Well, that was good. He looked at her, curled up, heaving. They called *him* the Bear. Hah.

Something else now, though. Something else about the dream.

He had seen the murder scene so clearly in it. The bright moon in a cloudless night sky. The bare trees in the park. And the stream, the sparkling stream, reflective, beautifully ominous in the moonlight. . . .

And the shoes . . .

My God.

"Huh," said Edwards, just audibly in the bedroom dark.

EIGHT

It was late in the morning when Edwards finally called her in. Julian could see he looked troubled.

"The shoes were black, all right," said Edwards, "but last night I sat bolt-upright in bed, dreaming about those shoes."

He flipped purposefully back through the well-thumbed calendar on his desk. "The night of the murder, October seventh, there was a full moon and no clouds. I note the conditions as a matter of course in an investigation. Set the stage. I always do."

"So?"

"Think for a moment about black pumps, shiny black patent-leather pumps in bright moonlight, moonlight maybe even reflecting in a running stream. How do they look?"

For the first time, Julian made a concentrated

effort to picture Sarah Langley just as Edwards had asked. Not as a statistic but as a real person. She pictured Sarah running, terrified, out of control, through the dark.

She found she could hear the footfalls, the heavy, steady, heaving breathing; the rhythms, the syncopations, of disaster. The entire scene brightened, sharpened in her mind, and then a corner of it seized her heart.

She looked at Edwards. "Oh my God. The shoes look white."

Edwards stared out the window for a moment, then looked at Julian. "I could really see it." He shrugged. "Maybe that's how they work. They just get a powerful picture, so powerful they can begin to see the details. Sort of a dreaming in waking life."

And Julian felt some tickle of instinct. Something deep in her, some little bit of premise wiggling up. "You know," she said, "Hill could have found out as easily as you did, that it was a clear night with a full moon."

"He certainly could have," Edwards agreed.

"And he knew she died by that stream. The pictures did show him that." Julian looked skeptically at the Chief. "Why are you giving him so much credit so quickly?" she asked, surprised to hear herself saying it. It was almost as if Edwards

knew, instead of merely suspected, that Hill was
genuinely on to something.

Edwards looked soberly at her over his bifocals. "I just want to be thorough, is all. I've always
been thorough, and I don't intend to stop now."

NINE

Julian was awakened by the slam of a door down the hall. The Ramada was usually silent as a tomb, had just a few regular tenants, and by now she could recognize almost every one of them. This slammed door wasn't typical of any of them.

The clock said three A.M. Julian knew almost without looking the cause of the sound. She knew what she would find. She dreaded looking. But she was, after all, a provisional officer of the law, and so it was her sworn duty to.

She pulled her trench coat over her nightshirt—that seemed easiest—and opened her hotel-room door.

The hall light was harsh: a bare high-wattage bulb casting its bland, unfocused institutional glaze over the hallway. And standing beneath it—at the end of the hall, bathed in the bulb's harshness, regarding it, and muttering arcanely to himself—was Wayne Hill.

She looked carefully, hoping for some clue, some indication, of whether this was authenticity or charlatanism—a show carefully mounted for her benefit at three A.M.

Silently, she drew closer, trying to make out the words, but he stopped, of course, as she got closer.

He looked up, startled.

"Mr. Hill."

"Oh, Miss Palmer." He smiled graciously.

She was sure he knew perfectly well that she was staying here on this hallway with him.

"Everything okay?" she asked.

"Hmm? Oh, sure. I was just getting ice from the ice machine, which isn't working for some reason, and, well . . . I was just mumbling curses at the damn thing. Forgive me. Although I did manage to at least get something out of it."

Whereupon he displayed the sorry quarter-cup of ice in the red Coke cup.

And it suddenly occurred to Julian: That *was* all he was doing. That was it. Getting ice. Nothing more.

She had expected to find him studying his hands, speaking in tongues . . .

There was such a thing as too much suspicion.

Sensing plots everywhere. She'd seen some of her classmates fall rapturous victims to it. Captives of their own imaginations. She smiled to herself.

Wayne Hill suddenly looked stricken. "I didn't wake you, did I? Oh dear," he said quaintly. "I . . . I'm sorry if I woke you. I did assume, of course, you were down the hall, and I . . . I should have been quieter. But that damn ice machine . . . I'm sorry."

"That's okay," she smiled—at him, at herself. "That's okay. It really is."

If he was a charlatan, he certainly had the most complete act imaginable, and she had to give him credit for that, at least.

In a suddenly playful shift of mood, Wayne Hill looked her up and down, and from within his shambling, slouching, adamantly and willfully strange self, there came into his eyes for a moment the sparkle of a sexual being. "Do you always sleep in your trench coat?" he teased.

"No, but I always investigate in it."

He seemed poised to continue, but—just as in the station house—some formality, some protective wall, slammed down, and he literally, almost visibly, seemed to change his mind.

"Good night, Miss Palmer," he said suddenly, leering frozenly.

"Good night, Mr. Hill."

And he headed back, presumably, toward his room.

But because Julian had asked the desk clerk, out of curiosity and precaution, what room Hill was in, she knew he was now headed in the wrong direction.

"Mr. Hill?"

He looked up.

"Aren't you in one thirty-two?"

"Yes."

"But it's . . . it's that way."

He looked up. "So it is," he said with a smile. "Not much of a psychic at three A.M. But who is?" And he switched direction.

TEN

The next morning began badly.

Julian arrived promptly at nine to find Mr. Hill, scrubbed, fresh-looking, wearing what was clearly a brand-new suit with a ridiculous pink pocket square (the only pink pocket square, certainly, within hundreds of miles), appearing far from destitute—indeed appearing like an entirely different person—and ensconced in the outer office, at Julian's desk, in fact, giving an interview to what Julian quickly gathered was a reporter from the *Albany Mail*.

She crossed the station-house floor in a gathering fury. How naive she'd been! This, of course, was what came with a psychic. She caught raspy-voiced but proud phrases coming at her across the station-house floor. ". . . began working on it yesterday . . . not at liberty to say at this moment. . . .

Yes, something the investigation did not have before . . ."

Julian was stunned. "What's going on! Where did you get that—"

"This is Miss Palmer," said Hill, coolly attempting to head her off with an introduction, "who is assisting—"

There was a bellow from behind them.

"Ah, Chief Edwards," said the *Albany Mail* reporter, who—Julian saw instantly—knew perfectly well the wrath that would be incurred.

"Interview over, Arthur," Edwards said firmly to the reporter, "Mr. Hill, if you would . . ." He gestured him, with a sweeping arm and exaggerated gentility, into his office, barely containing his rage.

Edwards had been consummately professional, cordial, even gentle, since that morning he had rudely discovered her gender. He had managed to largely contain his displeasure over the removal of the photographs. But she could see in the clenched fists, the color suddenly rushing over the massive epidermis, that the legendary wrath was lurking there all the time. That it had only been slumbering, waiting for an excuse to awaken, a reason to rear up again, and now it had a good one.

Wayne Hill had hardly sat down before the Great Chief was hovering over him, his bulbous detective's nose suspended above Hill's. "You got your nerve"—the four words said low, spaced evenly, precisely, barely controlled.

"Well, gee, I mean, they called—"

"WHAT THE HELL ARE YOU DOING?!"

Julian felt her body tighten. She heard the glass partition rattle and resonate with the vibration of Edwards' vocal fury.

"Now, wait a second," said Hill, struggling to gather his forces, "it's a free press, and they have a right to—"

"Not *my* investigation," said Edwards summarily, "and don't try using *him*"—gesturing generally in the direction of the *Albany Mail* reporter—"to pressure *me* into committing to *you*." His jabbing finger punctuated thickly and threateningly. It seemed it could land with the force of a shotgun cartridge.

Hill was silent, caught. Then he smiled. "I know what this is about." He looked up impishly at Edwards. "You're embarrassed. Embarrassed by the services of someone like me—"

"You don't talk to him again," Edwards fumed, cutting him off. "We are working on a murder here, not selling newspapers." Edwards squinted. "What's with the suit?"

Hill smiled brazenly at him again. "Well, we

both know you *will* be using me, so it's just a little advance—"

Edwards slammed his fist on his desk. Files, pencils, tape, scissors, jumped in uniform obedience. He looked out the window to Rhine Brothers Hardware. Breathed deeply. Sat down. And looked Hill directly in the eyes.

"Because of guys like that," he said, calming only slightly to explain, gesturing through the glass partition to Art, who was leaning against a doorjamb across the station-house floor, "I still don't know if Wayne Hill, Psychic, is Wayne Hill, Con Man, don't you see?" He looked full at Hill. "The things you told us yesterday were in the papers."

"Really? I don't read the papers."

Edwards' face dropped all expression, went blank.

"You . . . you don't read the papers. At all?"

Hill shook his head no.

"Never read anything about this case?"

"Why, no."

"But didn't you say you read about it in the papers?"

"I said I knew it was *in* the papers."

"But you knew Sarah Langley's name."

"Well, yeah, I mean . . . it came to me."

"It came to you."

"That's what I'm doing here, after all," Hill said without irony.

"It came to you." Edwards, it seemed, could only, for the moment, repeat it. It was a tough concept to grasp.

"In my room. I was looking out the window at the trees." Hill seemed about to explain more, to testify to the sensation, to the transmission and arrival of the knowledge, to its route, to how it came to hover above the treeline, but then he seemed abruptly—yet again—to abandon the effort. "Look, that's the only reason I called. Because I knew."

"You expect me to believe that?"

"Yes," said Wayne Hill, palms open and eyes clear.

Edwards leaned back in the enormous ancient chair. "What is it?" said Edwards. "How does it work?"

Hill smiled, resigned.

Julian could see that, for Wayne Hill, it was an enormous gulf, a chasm that would never be bridged. He was on one side, and the world was on the other. Or at least that was the impression he conveyed. "You should read a few descriptions of psychics trying to explain what they feel, what happens." He smiled. "It's ridiculous. *Enquirer* stuff. Alternate universes. Currents. Soul-plasm in the ionosphere. Good Christ. You'd have me out of this office so fast—" He looked at Julian as well as Edwards. "I don't like being laughed at. So I don't try to describe it. Figure if I just get results, I don't have to answer questions."

Julian wanted more. Much more. She knew Edwards did, too. They were people who had to know. Detectives, after all. Julian knew that Hill could do much better than this. Or at least stumble around a bit more trying. He could ingratiate himself so well with them, simply by making the effort, but he wasn't going to. As if they could never understand. It was so arrogant. They wanted more. But no more was forthcoming.

Edwards looked blankly at Hill.

"It's different from anything else in our experience," Hill said. "And you can ask Madame Tara and Jeanne Dixon all you want about it, but with me, you're gonna have to leave it at that."

Edwards looked openly skeptical.

"Look, let's try to work a little again, all right? Let me try to help here. Bring in the photographs again, if you would. No special presentation. I've already touched them."

Wayne Hill, Psychic and Regular Guy. They didn't come any smoother, thought Julian.

*   *   *

Julian dumped the huge envelope on Edwards' desk.

With the exquisite care of an artist handling a masterpiece or a fragile relic, strange hands working delicately, Hill withdrew the photographs from the envelope.

Odd, considering how he'd riffled through them the first time.

Or were these changes of technique shrewdly calculated to keep them guessing about him? She couldn't decide yet. And decided that she *wouldn't* decide yet. She was learning to be a detective, so she'd do the detectively thing and wait for more evidence.

Julian had no wish to look at the photographs so closely again. But she did notice that Hill ran the nub of his missing finger, almost lovingly, across each photograph's surface.

Julian could not help it. She watched again as Sarah Langley's dismembered torso, her arms, her head, were glossily displayed anew.

She watched Edwards look again at the photographs, still searching them, it seemed, for clues. Satisfied, somehow, to be examining them again.

Hill continued looking closely, almost dispassionately fascinated, as if studying works of art.

"Well?" asked Edwards finally, impatiently.

Hill held up a hand—his better hand—to quiet him.

Not a good thing, to hush Winston Edwards.

The silent examination went on a short while longer.

"So?" said Edwards again, more impatiently.

Hill looked up. "I'm not getting anything."

Oh brother.

"There's something—I don't know—blocking me . . ."

Oh, you poor bastard, you don't know who you're dealing with here, thought Julian.

"Look, can I take these outside for a minute?" Hill said it so fast that Edwards had no chance to react, except to wave his hands.

And Julian—fearing the Chief's gathering rage and wanting to get out of that office, which she felt sure was about to explode—offered suddenly: "Sure, um, good idea, come with me," hardly realizing she had said it.

In an instant, Julian and Hill were on the steps, out in the biting breeze, out in the crisp November air, just heading down the steps, when Wayne Hill, apropos of nothing, looked up at Julian and said, "A scarf. A blue scarf." He looked at his hands, his missing finger, then up at Julian again, and smiled.

"Mr. Hill," Julian responded, "I think we'd best call it a day. The reporter thing really took it out of him."

"The Ramada again?" he asked hopefully.

Julian actually felt sorry for the man. Whatever he was, genuine psychic or clever fraud, she sensed that beneath his occasional self-destructive challenges to the Chief, Wayne Hill was desperate, nervous, consumed with where he would be getting his next meal and spending his next night. His bright new suit already managed to appear somehow tattered. Julian reached in her pocket and fished out a five she had put there for lunch. "Here. Go over to Rhine Brothers and get yourself something. We'll get back to you."

She found Edwards standing at the window; he could have been staring at the two of them, witnessing the whole scene, or perhaps he was just staring out. He seemed a little calmer.

She'd been surprised at the quickness and degree of Edwards' anger. It had felt far out of proportion to the threat of Hill's vain loquaciousness with the reporter—a threat which hadn't had a chance to materialize anyway.

"Thanks for getting him out of here. You do indeed have instincts, Miz Palmer, and they are very good."

She smiled demurely.

"Have anything to say for himself?" Edwards asked, coming back now to his enormous ancient desk.

"Yes, actually," Julian said. She'd almost forgotten, she noticed, in her relief at having Hill out of here. "He said . . . What was it? Oh yeah. A blue scarf."

Edwards sat heavily, as always, into his chair. She wasn't sure he'd heard her.

He stayed with his head bowed at the desk for a moment. Then took a key from a janitorial keyring in the top desk drawer, opened the lock on one of the ancient brown file drawers behind him, slid open the file drawer, and took from it and tossed at her a piece of ripped fabric. Blue. Sparkled. "Found on a branch fifty yards from the scene. No label. A dozen mills run it, a thousand possible retail outlets for a scarf like that. Miz Palmer," he said heavily, "that's the clue I held back. From the newspapers. From the reports. That's the clue I held back from everywhere."

She watched him lean impossibly far back in the chair, regarded again his seeming defiance of physical laws. But now she heard a little more, got a little peek, at the defiance of other laws she had surmised that first day.

"Holding back. Little thing I'm sure they tell you about at the Academy, even if they don't condone it," said Edwards. "We do it, as you know, to let the criminal at large think he's more ahead of us than he is, to force a mistake or a drunken brag. You'd be amazed how often it works. But I've often asked myself if I do it more for the vanity of being the one to solve the case myself. You might not know it, but under these two hundred sixty–some-odd pounds and shabby suits, I've got my vanities."

Julian smiled politely in response.

Was Hill truly psychic? Was it possible? Here, finally, was a clue that, according to Edwards, couldn't come from anywhere else. The forty-six wounds, the white shoes, had other possible explanations. The blue scarf was different. It meant genuine psychic ability, or . . .

Julian thought, of course, of the other possibility, a dusty mote, a low, single off-key note in the humming of her consciousness. And if that other, dark possibility proved to be more than a mere possibility, then why—why on earth—was Wayne Hill here helping them?

"You as confused as I am?" asked Winston Edwards.

Julian smiled. Now Edwards was psychic. "We're only confused because we don't really believe in psychic ability," Julian ventured quietly.

"Time has come to get some answers," said Chief Edwards. "You get on that phone, make two calls. One: call the Ramada, tell Mr. Hill to keep himself fed and amused as economically as possible, please, while you and I, tell him, are away on some police business. Two: call U.S. Air and get us flights first thing tomorrow morning Albany to Raleigh-Durham, North Carolina."

"Raleigh-Durham? Wha—"

"Duke University. Country's foremost center for the legitimate study of parapsychology."

"But will they—"

"They know we're comin'."

Julian stood up, astonished.

"Well, you don't think I've been sittin' in here shufflin' papers, do you?"

ELEVEN

In November, North Carolina was a transforming pleasure, compared with upstate New York. The university was beautiful. Rich vestiges of autumn surrounded them on the drive from the airport to the school, and Julian wondered briefly if, upon her own graduation, this would be an area worth looking for work, but quickly banished the thought. *Too close. Too painful.*

The return flights were mornings at nine A.M. and early afternoon. Which meant, of course, that they would have to spend the night. It occurred to Julian that they would have dinner out. A nice dinner out. She felt herself looking forward to that.

"Come in, come in," said Professor Alain Le-Compte, one of the directors of the parapsychology program. He said in his mild but distinct French accent, "We are always so pleased to welcome our friends in law enforcement."

"Well, I'll admit I never thought I'd be here. This is Julian Palmer, my Associate trainee."

"Charmed," smiled LeCompte. "I'm sure, of course, it is a big step—no?—to visit us here. Let me show you what we do, I hope it will be useful."

The tour lasted precisely a half hour, and it was, upon reflection, one of the most remarkable half hours that Julian had ever spent. It was not the various tests being administered by young researchers in a series of rooms on the top two floors of this beautiful gothic building, projectors and flash cards and household objects on starch-clean white tables—these she had fully expected to see. Rather, it was the details: the lead shields in the walls between the rooms, the antistatic switches and carpeting; the sophisticated and eerily effective sound-baffling; the silent but immense ionizing machines in a closet at the end of every hallway, which lent the flow of words that passed from LeCompte, the comments that passed between them, and even the air they breathed a science-fictive otherworldliness. She would be, in that remarkable half hour, overwhelmed by a single and startling thought: *Jesus. This is serious.*

In LeCompte's generous office, overlooking a broad lawn and gothic roofs and ivy creeping like a cat burglar up and along the hewn-stone flanks of the building, the discussion got quickly to the point.

"When all is done and said—said and done, yes?—psychic ability is like any other ability. One does not either have it or not have it. But rather, some have more of it, and some have less of it. Here we have been able to quantify quite accurately and convincingly that some have more and some have less. But we have not explained yet satisfactorily why, or where it comes from. Some people have some. Some have none. And some people"—LeCompte looked suddenly very serious—"are off the chart."

From a drawer behind him, he took a file. "Your man, Wayne Hill. We have had him here."

Clearly this was news to Edwards. "You have?" he said.

"Oh yes. After the famous Pike Twin murders, and his assist on the Church Bell murder."

"And?" Edwards, Julian saw, was no longer the polite and cordial parapsychological tourist. He was alert, impatient now. His graciousness evaporated like a morning mist.

"We put him through a battery of five tests. The tests used, reserved for only the most talented, those with the most extreme—"

"Yes, yes, yes, Professor. And how did he do?"

LeCompte, slightly offended, answered anyway. "He demonstrated not the slightest psychic ability on any of them."

Only a test, of course, not necessarily conclusive, interruptive mechanisms possible . . . Alain LeCompte called out disclaimers in a desperate verbal jumble, as Winston Edwards stomped out the door, Julian barely keeping up.

They sat at dinner, in a restaurant that was part Saturday-night candlelit romance, part dark tavern. The conversation was a good bit more intensive than she had anticipated.

"Good cadet that you are, I'm sure you've been mulling over the same two possibilities I have," Edwards said somberly, cutting vigorously into his steak. "A: That we are dealing with someone of genuine and considerable psychic ability. A thesis that, while still possible, was cast sorely into doubt by our discoveries of today. And B . . . Miz Palmer?" He looked at her. "I want to hear it from you. Possibility B?"

She was surprised to feel the words catch in her throat. "B: That Wayne Hill killed Sarah Langley."

They were silent for a moment, listening to the sentence, the thought, hang in the air, silent while each considered the ramifications. They both had been thinking it for some time, of course. Now it was said aloud.

"Which doesn't do much to explain why he's volunteered to help find her killer," Julian added.

"Well, if we're dealing with that kind of maniac, there's no assigning reason to it," said Edwards. "I mean, I'm sure there's a reason; it just won't be readily fathomable by conventionally reasonable people."

Southern Muzak emanated from the restaurant's interior darknesses, a manufactured twang, ingenious in its inspecificity, a musical master of disguise, a musical spy.

The Bear took a swig from his mug of beer, tiny in his hand. "I suppose it would make more than a little sense at this point to look more into the case that Mr. Hill wasn't able to solve upstate. The one where he, uh . . . lost his power."

It had occurred to Julian, too, of course. The fact that Hill's powers had suddenly, inexplicably failed on a murder investigation a year ago, coupled with the fact that his clues so far on this one were so unerringly and eerily accurate.

They looked at each other.

Who knew if other murders had come in between? There was a sufficiently fat file of unsolved murders in upper New York State. Julian had seen it.

"We should call now, shouldn't we?"

Edwards looked up over his bifocals. "What for? Mr. Hill is sitting contentedly in our Ramada. He'll be there when we get back. And all we've got is speculation. If there'd been enough evidence to act before, my friend Chief Richards over in Northward would have had him, believe me."

They ate silently.

"But why?" Julian suddenly felt compelled to ask the wise old Bear a few moments later, with an innocent directness that dropped all big-city pretense, all the sophisticated gloss of her Academy years, abandoned in a single moment. "Why would a man who was once the solution, slip across somehow, I guess . . . slip across, to become the problem?"

Edwards cocked his head and studied the golden liquid of the beer glass. Julian took the opportunity, in turn, to study Edwards. His glasses refracted the candlelight.

He seemed to her sometimes oddly delicate, cautious, professorial—and other times, simply, mutely, a man-mountain. That was at least part of his strange appeal. He seemed a place, a place as much as a person; a piece of terrain, secure, immutable, predictable as land itself. A mountain, breathing with life. And as Canaanville was becoming steadily, physically colder, day by day, he contained, somehow, warmth enough to countermand it.

"He got so close, so fast, to police work," said Edwards of Hill. He looked deeper into the mug. "Some pretty dramatic police work, after all. Maybe he found it ... I don't know ... alluring. Maybe it swept him up somehow, he identified with the criminal—another outsider, after all."

He washed the beer around the glass, watched the golden centrifugal chase. "The ability to solve those earlier crimes—the Pike Twin murders, the Church Bell homicide—involved *feeling* the crime in some way, and maybe the feeling was ... well, intoxicating." He looked up, and his look seemed to say that he both doubted what he'd just said and knew something in it was true.

And even *she* could understand, at this moment, that sense of allure, of intoxication. For, on just a glass of wine, and a candelit dining room, and a police legend across the table taking her seriously, and a thesis between them as savory in its way as the meal, she, too, was feeling intoxicated, alive, herself.

"Meaning, maybe, that Wayne Hill *could* have solved the one he supposedly lost his ability on," said Julian slowly, putting it together. "But he wanted—*needed*, more than that—to try his own hand at it," she continued ruminatively. "You think?"

"I could see it," said the Chief offhandedly, almost cheerfully. "Particularly if he thought he saw a way to pull it off undetected."

"Meaning, perfect. A Perfect Crime." She smiled at him.

He paused. Flattered, she thought, that she had remembered. "Yes," he said, finally responding. "A Perfect Crime."

But he looked a little bothered, she noticed. "Something's troubling you, though."

"Good instincts again, Miz Palmer," he said, this time without smiling. "You'll laugh."

"Go ahead."

"Wayne himself says that he had lost the ability, but now it's returned." Edwards looked at Julian. "Isn't that possible, after all? That he *did* lose the ability, was indeed of no use on those subsequent cases, and was tested down here while it was lost, and now it *has* returned?"

"You're putting me on," said Julian.

Indeed this was either a foolish detective or a thorough one, she thought. How could he still grant Wayne Hill all this leeway, all this credit? After hearing of Hill's failure with LeCompte, after the finicky, coy, teasing dangle of the white shoes and blue scarf clues, after Hill's sometimes desperate, sometimes acquisitive, sometimes nakedly publicity-hungry behavior, even after discussing with her the other unsolved murder that Hill was associated with, Edwards was still entertaining the notion of Hill's psychic ability. "I have to tell you, Chief, I find it hard to believe that you're still toying with that idea."

He spoke instructively. "Because it is a possibility. I heard what Dr. LeCompte said at the very end, even if it seemed like I didn't."

"I also know what you really thought of the good Doctor."

They both smiled.

He took another bite, looked up at her. "But having sorted through some of Wayne Hill's possible motivations, there's another motivation in all this that baffles me."

"What's that?"

"Yours."

This took her by surprise. "What do you mean? I . . . I want to solve the crime. . . ."

He leaned back. "What is it about you, Julian? What did that impressive resumé leave off?" He examined his mug of beer again, as if seeing it for the first time, from a new angle. "Your looks. Your brains. You could have done anything, and we both know that. Police work wouldn't be the natural choice. There's something else to it, isn't there?"

Julian was silent. Edwards looked back at her, and now seemed to gaze into her, as he had that first day, when he'd assessed so accurately the contents of her briefcase, the precise date of her haircut, the vintage of her suit, and even her masturbatory morning. He studied her eyes again the same way now. "You're escaping something. That much I know. The way you wear your sophistication, and your education, and your big-city cynicism. It's all just a little too new. All just a little too eager. Like you're cloaked in it to disguise yourself. To hide from something. You're ill at ease in Canaanville, I can see that—cynical, annoyed with it, and yet somehow comfortable, familiar with it, too." He leaned forward almost imperceptibly. "You know, I've figured for a while now you're from a small town just like it. Aren't you? And here you are back in a small town, and you hate being back, and yet you love being back."

She looked away from him. Of course, by her looking away, he would know he was right.

"But something more," he said. "See, there were other possible escapes for you. But there's something about police work. I see it in you. A sense of mission. Zeal. Your interest in this case. Your emotional investment. And choosing to intern with a notoriously difficult chief. Why?"

She shrugged, but her shrug did not shake off his gaze. "Righting some wrong," he said, squinting into the beer glass. "Seeking justice. I've seen that before, of course, in lots of people in this line of work. But it must be such a strong pull, luring you in from other possible lives." His eyes narrowed. "Something happened. Something big. For which you're still searching for restitution."

He looked at her, smiling a brief, forced, cursory smile. "I see no flash of dispute in your eyes. No protest to any of this. Which tells me you're going along with it, somehow. Riding with its truth. So I'll go on." He looked at her. "Now, a hunch. A hunch based on thirty years at this. A hunch, and a leap. Ready?"

No. Yes.

"Someone was murdered in your small town, weren't they?"

The insipid music echoed from the walls of the small dark restaurant. Music, walls, that seemed to close in.

She nodded.

He paused. Cocked his head suddenly—a slight but physical reception to the shock of a new thought. "Someone you knew."

She looked at him. She felt a pleading, a pleading and cry at once familiar and yet from some place so deep within her that only in rare moments in her life was she aware of it, a place of despairing and yawning darkness; and in those rare moments, it snuck out of her, escaped her as she had sought to escape it, and revealed itself and her in that pleading look. She felt the pleading look escape her now, and knew that Edwards saw it, because she saw his eyes go suddenly, marginally wider, a diameter of recognition, of everything falling into place, and then, clearly, he knew.

"Your father," he said.

The music played insolently.

He waited, looked at her, and in a moment, quietly added the final, inevitable chord of explanation.

"Unsolved."

Julian sat immobile.

The world stopped.

A door. Footfalls. Blackness. The creak of the springs, the breathing of her sister asleep in the

*bunk above her. A bowl smashes. A thump. Silence.
A scream. Sirens.*

*Frozen. Frozen in the bed. Immobilized. Amid
the choking heat, the pooling sweat, the new rise
of screams, frozen. Immobilized.*

*The door flung open. The sheriff filling the
doorway. "Get up, girls."*

No, I can't.

*Pulling them, prying them up. Her sister
screaming. Her, frozen.*

*Holding the knife. The sheriff. In plastic. The
knife.*

*Into the fray. Red cherry light sweeping doom
across the kitchen. The pounding of uniformed
boots and her own heart, the sudden bright flood
of light after the bedroom dark, the indecipherable
crackle of the radios; and men, men, nameless,
faceless, looking through her nightie at the first
bloom of her breasts; two who smile at the warmth
and wetness of urine down her leg. A man's laugh
in the other room; and over it all, dominating it
all, more powerful even than the wail of her
mother, her mother, always silent, wailing, wailing
now incalculably, yet most powerful of all, in the
middle of the floor, the lump of body beneath the
tarp, like a sack of sand. The howl of the gods. The
smirk of the fates. Senseless. Brutal.*

A frantic, crescendoing crackle of radios. The

rush of exit. Quickness to the trail. The evaporation of disaster. Instant. Dreamlike. Unreal.

But the trail had stopped. Hundreds, thousands of unsolved murders. Every state had its thick files of them. And that was that. A federal shrug. A governmental show of concern. A continuation of life in the Sheriff's Office. Parking tickets. Overdue taxes. Disturbing the peace.

The trail had stopped. And where the trail had stopped, the unraveling had begun.

Frozen. Frozen in the bed. Freezing out the memory. Freezing it in.

She realized, in a moment, that Edwards was leaned forward, looking at his plate, searching it. "You became the man then, didn't you?" he said. *Yes—why yes, that was right.* "Someone had to be strong, had to be a man emotionally, and it fell to you." He tapped a huge finger reflectively, pensively, pausing between taps. "The impersonation of a man on your resumé. To cynically make a point, sure, but it turns out there's truth to it, too, isn't there? Psychological truth." He studied the golden liquid in his glass one last time. Studied it, it seemed, so as not to look at her.

"The murder of your father," he said, the words

flat, frank, factual; no less, no more. "Your real resumé."

From the restaurant's dark corners, the bland recorded music continued—blithe, unaware, mildly twinkling, happy.

"It finished us," Julian said quietly, her voice strange to herself, hearing it at last. "It destroyed us. Our family. Splintered us. Scattered us. I'm alone now. Have always been." The feeling welled, and she pushed it down. She was harder *and* softer than those around her. She had known that, had seen that in herself forever. Her cynicism and snideness were fear and doubt. Harder and softer. "The town, by the way? Just a hundred miles from here," she added ruefully.

"So even your accent is gone," observed Edwards, a small, grim afterthought.

What more could be said? What could be added, or changed? In the wake of the moment, there could only be a respectful quiet. And then, with no other choice, each adopted a ruse of normality. In the next minutes—those of finishing the meal, paying the bill, finding a cab, and brushing through the dense fragrant warm autumn night—life went on. But carefully, tentatively, fragilely.

"It's not the Ramada, but I hope it'll do," he

said, when they were checked in, and stood with their bags at the doors of their respective rooms, which faced each other across the hall. They seemed to be the only two guests, and if that proved to be the case, she wouldn't be all that surprised. Who else would be here?

"Flight time again?" he asked.

"Nine A.M.," she reminded him. "We should leave here eight the latest."

"Well, okay, then," said the Chief awkwardly, looking at her, turning away, looking up the hall, then at her again, then reaching down to heft his bag off the floor. "Well, okay. Good night," he said, looking over his bifocals one more time, and then suddenly shoving them tightly on his nose, as if to erase the troubling and enticing vision filling them.

"Good night," she said back.

Exhausted, wrung-out, Julian Palmer stripped physically as briskly and as completely as she had been emotionally stripped just a half hour before. She pulled off her blue skirt, her white blouse, unhooked her bra, and let her round, firm, too-large breasts tumble out in thankful freedom and escape. She slid her panties off her too-slim hips, slipped the pins from her black hair to let it cascade onto her shoulders, and stood in front of the hotel room's full-length mirror.

The familiar recognition, the familiar thought: Here was what the commotion was about. What the electric eyes, the ball-bearing necks, the uncomfortable, magnetized shifts of posture, had been about—in junior high, high school, on the familiar streets of her little town, at the Academy, and now with Simms and the others in the Canaanville station. This—in the mirror in front of her—would also in some way turn out to be, she knew, why Sarah Langley was dead.

But now, an unfamiliar notion, something new: That the stripping was more complete. She was barer, somehow. More naked. Sexier because of it. It seemed to be more herself there in the mirror. The curves and shapes more recognizable. More her. *The Bear. The Barer*, she thought.

What was it about him? She'd been examining it for a while now. Certainly nothing physical. The man was immense. Far older. Beaten-down–looking even beyond his years. His craggy, jowly face was practically comical in its weatheredness. He had about him—in his whole personality—a kind of magnificent sloppiness. So what was it, exactly?

It was a lot of things, she'd concluded before tonight. A list of things that she'd assembled, rational, comprehensible. How a familiarity, an intimacy, never had to build. How it had existed from the first interview, from the moment he'd mentioned her masturbation. And that moment—left unexplored, un–expanded-upon—had oddly planted an intimacy silently but surely into place.

And the power. Complete control over those around him. How they cowered. Initially repulsive to her. But she saw that it derived naturally, from his natural force, not from threat. It came from the authority he brought to the position, not from the position itself. Brusque, offhand power. Incidental. Uncalculated.

The total control of a town. And, if it was a small town, a tiny domain, the control was still total. And something in that control, that supreme authority, the despotic potential, the exercise of his own rules—something in all that was intriguing to her. With the freedom, the command, the confidence that the body in the mirror provided, she herself had never been totally controlled, and she was . . . well, curious about it. Curious on a physical level. Stirred up by it. She knew herself, and had to admit that.

But tonight, what she had been resisting became sharp and crisp and undeniable. That the power, the control, weren't it at all. If they played any part, it was a small one.

It was, instead, his talent. A police talent so

enormous, so intuitive, that his looks, his brusque manner, his sometime silence, his boorishness, all were secondary; in fact, they placed the talent in even greater, higher relief. Maybe it should be called genius; genius which so often was eccentric, irascible, uncooperative, apart; genius that kept him consigned to a backwater, incapable of working with others, of getting along with employees or bosses. Genius—the kind they spoke of hushed and late in the dorm halls at the Academy. The small handful of names tossed around in wee-hour discussions: Pumin in Oswego, McMalley in the South Bronx, Edwards in Canaanville. The Academy frowned on such idolatry—police work was a matter of science, not personality. Yet it was the very unofficialness, the lack of sanction of the dormitory talk, and the fabled eccentricities attached to each name that let them melt into myth on reverent trainee tongues.

Enormous, nearly inexplicable ability. And she was a sucker for it. The world she knew had been, in mere moments, thoroughly shattered, and in the infinitely colder and more rugged world that took its place, there was no family, no resources, no filial privilege. And in this more rugged world, talent and ability were all she had, all she could fall back on, all she could turn to, or trust.

It was his talent. Pure talent that overrode his

insolence and his parochialism. *Police* talent. And she understood the added allure of that, because there was, after all, a crime that she still wanted solved. And Winston Edwards, in a strange way, might have talent enough to solve it.

She'd thought it as he spoke tonight. As they had sat there silently afterward. It was obvious. She wasn't naive. Though its obviousness didn't seem to lessen its power. She had lost a father. And here, in a way, she had found one.

Old, wise. Secure. A place. The man who would solve the unsolved. If not the original crime, then at least the promise of some liberation and release in solving this one. And others. She fully recognized the dose of seductiveness the image brought to Edwards. She was sophisticated enough to know that this image of a father might in some way have been part of her attraction to Canaanville and the autocratic, singular, mythic Winston Edwards. Part of her choice—and why she had so easily ignored the advice of her classmates and so smoothly shut out her own doubts.

Her thoughts turned vaguely to Mrs. Edwards. The woman existed only as a ghostly figure in Julian's mind. To Julian, she was a cipher—Edwards, she had long noticed, never even mentioned her. Though Julian, for her part, had never asked or prompted. She felt Estelle Edwards only as a theoretical, moral force. Not, as Edwards would say, "a person, a life." But as a theoretical force, Julian found herself thinking about Estelle Edwards now.

In a life that had dealt her an enormously difficult hand, Julian had been supremely careful, had taken extreme measures—out of some blend of deep morality and simple courtesy—not to make life any more difficult for anyone else.

She suspected that Edwards had gone outside the marriage—his childish, unnecessary protestation at the Rhine Brothers lunch counter that first day, that he'd never been inside the Ramada. So the marriage wasn't good. Did that somehow excuse subsequent behavior? Make somehow acceptable whatever might come? She was a state-sworn upholder of the rules, liked that about herself. What would she do? In the eventuality . . .

She looked again at herself in the mirror. Who was that, exactly? That creature looking back—smooth, turned and curved to such effect.

They were both prisoners of their bodies, she had noticed. He, of one old and fading. She, of one that attracted such attention, it often felt as if it were not her own, but someone else's. It was a specific, physical identification with Edwards. They were both strangers in their own bodies, both sometimes frustrated by them, and this was something more, something further, they had in common.

The tour with LeCompte had left her both believing fully in psychic ability and not believing it at all. Made her sure, at least, that it didn't deserve the occult coloration or the arcane status. Because "psychic" seemed to her, in the end, to be only, well . . . an intensity of connection. A heavy dose of a capacity that existed variously in all of us. Wasn't that all it was? An intense connection, an intense focus of a certain sort?

Akin to intuition—which detectives had, after all, which made them detectives, drew them to the craft—and which they more modestly labeled instinct, hunch. Was that why detectives hated psychics, because they were up to the same game, really?

Was it this kind of intense connection that had drawn her here? Connection beyond the "reasons"? Beyond the literal?

Was that the lesson of the day?

Or the lesson of the night?

As she lay down on the bed, shifting on its lumpy mattress, staring up at the stucco ceiling, the thoughts all swirled together, a simmering cerebral stew, its ingredients blending at last into something desirable, anticipated, exciting.

Profound connection.

Of mind. Of spirit.

The allure of closure. Of solving more than a crime: solving, in a way, a life.

It was more than she had ever dared to hope from a tiny town in upstate New York administered by what was erroneously rumored to be a tyrannical police chief.

Enough bad had happened in her life already: it had to be behind her; the good had to be ahead. The odds—she smiled to herself in the dark—had to run overwhelming that way.

She shifted uncomfortably, hyped-up, excited, but smiled nevertheless and uncontrollably into the dark.

And at two in the morning, when she heard the shuffling down the hall, the crunch of the ice machine, she knew there was someone else who—like herself—couldn't sleep.

She thought, of course, of her three A.M. ice-machine encounter with Wayne Hill in Canaanville, but she had a quite different feeling about this figure rustling at the ice machine. Affection. Admiration. A sense of companionship. Of closure. All of that. At the very least.

The detective in her felt compelled to make another middle-of-the-night hallway investigation. Though, leaving her room this time, she felt comfortable enough, warm enough, at home enough, not to throw her trench coat on over her nightshirt, as she had done with Hill.

"Can't sleep?" she asked the hulking and eccentric but genial and somehow gentle man in the hall.

"Can't sleep."

"Me neither." *Dumb, dumb.* Her city wit, her quickness, abandoning her. *What am I doing here? What exactly am I doing here?* Suddenly aware of the chill in the hall.

Awkwardly, hugely, tentatively yet urgently, a bear-paw reaches out, presses its palm against her nightshirt and against the tight stomach beneath it. The tight stomach now tightens even more. . . .

She looks at him. "I . . . I just . . ." Then says it, cannot help but say it. "Estelle . . ."

The huge bear-head shakes a quick and urgent no. "Been over for years," he informs, factual, long past sadness.

In the dimly lit hallway, his limpid brown eyes seem to swirl with color.

She puts her own hand over his on her stomach, laces her fingers gently into the paw.

Then, firmly, pulls the paw away.

"I can't," she says, smiling palely, regretfully. "It's . . . it's not right. . . ."

A flash in his eyes. A sudden tense set of jaw.

A shocking bulge of veins in his neck and forehead.

The pressure on her laced fingers. Paralyzing pressure.

Jesus!

The huge bear-head turning quickly away, those eyes averted. Then, more slowly, back. A small nod. A skewed smile of disappointment, acceptance. "Christ, you're somethin' "—muttering it hoarsely, low.

The moment passes.

But something has been in it. Something in him far beyond natural frustration, momentary anger. Her body, her senses, telegraphing something. Unclear. Something below her consciousness, which doesn't at all fit tonight's portrait of Winston Edwards, of the candlelit dinner, of the subtle intuition, of the fatherly aspect, and which therefore, at the moment, can't be processed by her. Too unclear. Something that, left undefined and elusive, melts into nothing. But something her body—free beneath the nightshirt, inches from Edwards, thus alive, awake, aware; her beautiful listening tool, of long and competent epidermal communication— something her body is whispering. But something she cannot yet quite hear.

TWELVE

"So where were you?" asked Wayne Hill, in the Canaanville offices with them by midday.

"Police business."

Hill closed his eyes, and squinted. "Gothic buildings. Ivy creeping across their sandstone faces. Warmth. A university."

Julian Palmer and Winston Edwards looked at him in a moment of confusion, an injection of horror.

He opened his eyes and laughed. "Simms told me. The Duke parapsychology program. You're taking me seriously. But I hope not too," Hill said. "Occupational hazard to suspect a psychic, you know, happens all the time. Otherwise, how could he know what he does?"

Julian looked at Edwards. But Edwards—carefully—did not return the look.

"I don't have to be psychic, as they say," said Wayne Hill, with a sheepish grin, "to know you suspect me."

Edwards took the high road. "Wouldn't you, if you were us?"

"I suppose. And I suppose you'll continue to suspect me until the killer is caught," said Wayne Hill, looking at Edwards.

Edwards was silent.

"Just for the record, I was upstate, in the hospital, at the time of the murder. You can check that with my psychiatrist, Dr. Tibor."

"I believe you, Mr. Hill," said Edwards. "I believe you. So, let's proceed, shall we?"

Wayne Hill looked down quite suddenly—as if startled—at his hands, studying them.

Edwards and Julian waited, expectantly.

He looked up again, just as suddenly. "I . . . I felt so clear this morning. . . . Are you sure all the files have been cleared from this office?"

Julian feared the Bear's reaction. But once again the Bear surprised her. "That's all right, Mr. Hill. I've got a better idea. Why don't we head to Sarah Langley's apartment? You up to that?"

"High time," said Hill, looking at the Chief.

And as Hill waited for them outside the door, outside the glass partition, Edwards pulled the small photo of Sarah Langley out of his wallet, waved it in front of Julian. "Remember," he said. "Not a statistic. A real girl."

Edwards, Julian, and Wayne Hill stood crammed together in the cramped kitchenette of the tiny second-floor apartment where Sarah Langley had lived. On the chipped, broken cement steps outside, Hill had insisted on entering alone, and having a minute by himself in there. Julian had expected grumbling protest and irritation from Edwards, but instead he had, like a courtly butler, gestured Hill in.

"How long are you going to let this little charade go on?" Julian asked Edwards, once Hill had gone up. And instantly felt fearful of his hearing her testiness, the shortness in her words. She knew, just as instantly, where this new fear of hers had come from. From that moment—that moment witnessed in her senses—in the hotel hall in Raleigh-Durham.

"How long will I let it go on? Long as it takes, I guess," Edwards said.

"You mean, to have something definitive," she allowed him.

"To have something definitive"—though he said "definitive" rather vaguely, Julian noticed.

She looked out at Southside. The section of

town for which the most calls came in on the Canaanville station-house lines, the section to which the town's black-and-whites were most often summoned. Shantytown, Funkytown, there were a lot of names for Southside at the station. The Chief referred to it by none of these, but instead with a generalized groan.

Julian watched her own breath tumble acrobatically before her in the cold November air, and then, in step with Edwards, headed up after Hill.

The kitchenette was so small, and Edwards so immense, the tails of all three of their coats touched.

"So?" Edwards challenged Hill now. "Anything while we were out?"

"Just needed to set my meters," said Wayne Hill with an insolent grin, and he turned, held out his hands as if to warm them over an invisible fire, and then, with a sudden change of mood, a pall, a somberness suddenly summoned and surrounding him, began to move, slowly and systematically, around the kitchenette and into the rest of the apartment.

For the moment Edwards and Julian stayed in the kitchenette.

Julian could see that the place was untouched. There were still boxes of breakfast cereal on the counter—Count Chocula, Captain Crunch. Instinctively she had expected to see yellow police tape wrapping and demarcating everything, but she remembered soon enough it was Canaanville, and Edwards had his own way of doing things. Or of not doing them.

She opened the ancient refrigerator. Mustard, ketchup, a can of frozen juice still defrosting. An unopened can of diet soda.

Well, why be formal? Why not do things the Edwards way? When in Canaanville . . .

She took the unopened soda out of the refrigerator. Gestured to Edwards, *Do you mind?*

In answer, Edwards went across to the other side of the kitchenette, opened a tiny cabinet, and took down a glass.

Julian was amused that he would know so readily where the glasses were. "Gee, you sure know your way around here," she teased him casually.

His eyes narrowed. "We've been in here a dozen times," he said humorlessly, and walked into the living room. Julian followed him. She and Edwards looked at the clothes piled on the floor. " 'Least a dozen—well, plenty of times, anyway—and nothin'. Zip," Edwards continued. Together they looked out the dirty windows. "Just some young girl," said Edwards absently. "Just some young girl, tryin' to get by. 'Scuse me."

Edwards went around the corner, Julian assumed, to relieve himself. She could see through the mirror mounted on the hallway wall opposite, as Edwards sidled into the tiny bathroom, and stood at the toilet and began to heft his coat and unzip his trousers, without shutting the door. Then, in a short moment, he grunted low, turned to the door behind him to close it, and very purposefully, Julian noticed, lifted it on its hinge in order for it to close. Julian stood looking at the door, vaguely uncomfortable, as the torrent of Winston Edwards' urine hit the water in the bowl.

"So?" Edwards said again to Wayne Hill, cynically, impatient as Hill came back down the hallway.

Wayne Hill's hands were still riding on air. His brow was furrowed. "Something is blocking me."

Edwards rolled his eyes at Julian.

But always a clue when he needs it, thought Julian. *Always a clue when he needs it.*

"Something . . ." murmured Hill, "strange," and went silent again.

"Yeah?" prompted Edwards.

"It's, well . . . I'm getting . . . a police presence."

"Oh," said Edwards irritably, broadly sarcastic, annoyed. "A police presence? At the site of a murder investigation? How 'bout that!"

"That's not what I mean," Hill said mysteriously, watching his hands, not even aware, it seemed, of his own words.

He drifted into the bedroom.

Julian stood a few steps behind him, at the door. She could see the big, king-sized mattress on the floor. It literally filled the little bedroom, so there was just a tiny aisle on each side of it.

Hill's hands hovered over the bed. "I mean . . . well, I don't know what I mean." He looked blankly. "A police presence."

"Well, like I just told Julian, we been in here a dozen times," Edwards called casually from the living room. "That's what you get in a police investigation, Mr. Hill."

Hill's hands hovered over the bed. He studied them. "Yeah. I know," he said. "Too bad." He looked at Julian, shrugged, and dropped his hands.

On the way out, Edwards stopped to look at the park across the way. The park where Sarah Langley had been murdered.

"Ready for it?" he asked Wayne Hill.

She heard the challenge in Edwards' voice. As if coming off some subtle sort of victory. Eager to get it out of the way, to get to the still-murky bottom of Wayne Hill. She was all for it.

"Not today," said Hill meekly, almost pleading.

"We're right here, you know," said Edwards. Julian wanted as much as Edwards did to accelerate the pace of the whole enterprise.

Wayne Hill, Psychic, must have sensed the Chief's impatience only too well. "Okay, tomorrow, then, Chief Edwards," he said, surprising both the Chief and Julian with this sudden and spirited alacrity of cooperation. Though perhaps it was calculated, as many things with Wayne Hill seemed to be, to keep Edwards and Julian off balance and guessing.

"Tomorrow, the park," Hill said.

THIRTEEN

Winston and Estelle Edwards sat at dinner in their small Victorian dining room.

"So?" said Estelle, somewhat cautiously and somewhat challenging.

"So what?" he shot back.

"So you know 'so what.'"

"I've never talked about my work. In thirty years, Estelle, I've never talked about my work. And I see no reason to start now."

"But this is different," she said.

He felt sick.

"And why is this different? It's a murder investigation. I've had dozens. Why is this different?" he said irritably.

"Because it's unsolved," she said.

He was silent.

"And I just wonder if it's going to stay unsolved."

Angrily he pushed his plate away.

"You can't stop a wife from wondering. You can certainly understand a wife's wondering, can't you, if a murder her husband is investigating is going to stay unsolved or not?"

The rage, the familiar rage, rose up in Winston Edwards.

He waited for it to pass. Used the familiar tricks: counting the seconds, listening to the click of the dining room clock, staring—distantly, no longer hungry—at his still-steaming food.

Veterans' Park—a bequest of a nineteenth-century mill owner, Canaanville's last wealthy resident at his death in 1928 and now quite secure in that title, it seemed—effectively composed one broad border of Southside.

They pulled to the curb. Veterans' Park lay before them—broad, expansive, mostly wooded. "It's always surprised me there isn't more violent crime in this park," Winston Edwards said. "It's such a perfect place. Plenty of crime that way," pointing to Southside across the street, "but not much makes its way into the park."

"Well, I'm sure it's out of respect for our veterans," said Julian sarcastically.

"And *I'm* sure it's because nobody in Southside thinks to hide anything. Ready, Mr. Hill?"

"If you don't mind, I'd prefer to go on ahead a little, without you. You may follow me at fifty paces or so," he said officiously.

Julian could see Chief Edwards bristle. Someday, somehow, there'd be retribution for that, she knew. But Edwards nodded in accordance nevertheless.

Hill went out in front of them as they crossed into the park. As if they were out in the park on a stroll, letting their dog run ahead.

The November cold, flirting with Julian, teasing her with its gusts when she first arrived, had clamped down now, settled in for long months like a despicable but close relation. It was silent, ubiquitous; a solid cold, a permanent fixture of the park like a statue. A cold that had the permanence of stone.

She was glad, actually, to have the moment to hang back with Edwards. He had been fairly distant and uncomfortable with her since the evening in Raleigh-Durham. But whatever she had glimpsed in his reaction that night had by now receded somewhat in her consciousness, melted away, to where she could more coolly examine it.

A reaction from him of some sort was only natural, she'd concluded. She just hadn't thought it would be to the degree she had experienced. She was, truthfully, still a little nervous, on edge, about it. Out here, tramping across the field, she'd had the vague idea of talking to him about it, to defuse the moment, but what would she say exactly? He didn't quite invite that sort of conversation. Today, especially, he seemed to have shut down to her completely. She soon learned the reason why.

"She wants you to move in with us. Estelle. Take the barn apartment while you're here."

Tension poured through her body like liquid, spreading its poison as it went. "I see."

She could feel again, vividly, the thick fingers pressing against her stomach through the nightshirt. Her own fingers laced in his. The stew of feelings. The tug of inevitability.

"What do you want to do?" asked Edwards, attempting to be casual. Specifically not looking at her as they tramped across the field.

"I . . . I don't know."

Part of her wanted the chance, the chance that seemingly would be assured, to discover what it was she had vaguely detected—a lurking rage, an aggression beyond sexual bounds—yet another part of her already had dismissed it, thinking that she was a little too much, a little too completely, playing the detective. She had dismissed it—logically, or maybe a little afraid. She was formulating a reasoned, measured response to the Edwardses' invitation, and had turned toward Edwards to carefully deliver it, but she could see Edwards was no longer on the topic. He was studying Wayne Hill.

Hill had been walking along the streambed, along a stand of trees, had stopped suddenly, and now stood absolutely still, at a certain spot. He spun his head, with an almost birdlike energy, around the spot, looking every way.

"He's in the precise spot," said Winston Edwards quietly, evenly. "He's in the exact spot where the murder took place."

Drawing closer, they could hear Hill's breathing. It was low, measured, from some cavity deep within him.

Was he hyperventilating?

Hill held up his hands. He looked at his hands. He seemed to be studying the missing finger, each finger, the palm.

He raised them up suddenly above his head, still studying them, as if in graphic relief against the cold blue November sky.

He turned in place. He seemed fascinated with his hands. And his fascination carried strangely, inexplicably but inevitably, to Julian and Edwards, watching his hands too.

"It's . . ." Wayne Hill said, his raspy voice now even raspier, deeper within him, than Julian had imagined a voice could be. "It's . . . so cold here, isn't it?"—as if caught, surprised by it, a mild realization too late. ". . . so brutally cold. . . ."

It was all he could manage.

Wayne Hill collapsed suddenly into the muddy stream, facedown in the water, the thin crust of ice at its edge splintering with a high crack, the thick, cold mud splashing up around him.

Edwards and Julian leaped forward to help him.

FOURTEEN

"Never happened before," he said in the emergency room, wrapped in two thermal blankets.

Edwards shoved a coffee at him, and then, remembering he did not drink coffee, grunted and drew it away.

"That's . . . I'm so sorry. I . . . don't know. . . . That's never—"

"How are you feeling?" asked Edwards, solicitously.

He nodded.

"You catch your breath here a little, Mr. Hill. I'm going to step over there with Miz Palmer and have a chat."

"How's it going with you and Miss Palmer?" asked Wayne Hill suddenly, with an evil glint in his eye.

Edwards looked fearfully at him.

"Well, you don't have to be psychic to see that, either," said Hill.

"Quite a fall," said Julian.

"Lot of people know how to take a fall," said Edwards.

"But if you're gonna do it, why not take a fall onto the embankment? I mean, he actually could have drowned."

"He knew he wasn't going to drown with two police officers standing there. And the threat of drowning makes it pretty convincing. Maybe a necessary step for him, a necessary risk, with two such skeptical observers."

"And what about the spot, Chief, how he went right to it?"

"Yes, how about that?" said the Chief. He looked at her. Obviously they were both thinking about the more logical, gruesome, and highly unpsychic reason Hill might have gone right to it.

"But," she asked, lowering her voice, "why would he have been so brazen?"

"That is the question, isn't it?" said Edwards.

"What do you think he'll have to say?" she asked.

"What do you think?" the Chief said. "Nothing. A lot of nothing."

*   *   *

"You feel ready to talk?" asked Chief Edwards.

"I feel ready, but I'm afraid I've got nothing very useful. A lot of feeling; no facts."

Edwards looked up at Julian: *What did you expect?*

"Something. Something went on with me out there, and I can't explain it," said Hill. "Something . . ." he said, shaking his head in frustration, pursing his mouth in puzzlement. "I . . . I'm sorry . . ."

"Well, then, we'll see you back at—"

"Wait," Wayne Hill called out suddenly, and held up his hand with the missing finger. "Wait. Yes. Something green. Reflective. Jade. I don't know. A necklace? A jade necklace?"

She wanted to laugh. *The Case of the Blue Scarf. The Case of the Jade Necklace. This is ridiculous. How can you let him go on, Winston?*

Edwards was silent on the walk back.

"More evidence held back, Chief?"

Edwards smiled.

"Was there one? A necklace?"

"Well, none was found."

"So he was wrong," Julian shrugged.

"So it would appear," said Edwards, and lapsed into silence again.

He seemed, with each new performance of Wayne Hill's, to spiral further into his brooding, his depression. Why was he so insistent on getting Hill to play out the charade? Would anything really come from waiting, from holding back?

It was as if Edwards was still afraid the crime would never be solved, she thought. Perhaps he knew, sensed in some way beyond her inexperience, that the murder would never be pinned on Wayne Hill.

If that was what Edwards somehow sensed, was brooding about, was he right? Was it indeed possible they would never solve it? Was it indeed, as Edwards had suggested that second morning, to Julian's hidden cringing and suppressed laughter, a Perfect Crime?

She couldn't take another unsolved crime.

White shoes. A blue scarf. A jade necklace. Ceiling fans. Metal files. A psychic. A Perfect Crime. Good Christ.

It was becoming the bad movie of her first impression. A time warp. An unreality. And why the hell wouldn't Edwards shut off the projector?

FIFTEEN

Estelle Edwards began to press harder to have the new girl stay in the barn—it was positively uncivil to have her still lodged in that Ramada—and Edwards shifted so uncomfortably in his dinner chair that it squeaked and groaned in protest.

"Why? Why, Estelle? She's fine at the motel. It's comfortable, clean, nothin' wrong with it. . . ."

"What's wrong with having her here? I think we ought to."

"Estelle, why . . . why are you doing this? You know it makes me uncomfortable. . . ."

"Relax. Why should it? She's a nice girl, I'm sure. There's no problem, is there?" she said challengingly.

They looked at each other silently, across the tops of their eyeglasses.

Why was she doing this?

* * *

"Richie, I'm going to put you on the squawbox, so my new assistant can hear what you have to say."

Edwards switched the phone call to the speaker—another of those touches of modernity lurking beneath the dust. "Say g'morning to Julian Palmer," said Edwards.

"Hello, Julian," came the crackling greeting.

"It's Chief Richards," Edwards informed Julian, "my buddy in Northward."

"Hi, Chief Richards."

"Ah, a woman! How'd ya get so lucky, Winston?"

"Dumb luck," said Edwards, smiling at Julian. "Believe me. Dumb luck."

"Hell, this Associates Program got me John Simington, here with me now. Gee, John, you don't seem so terrific to me anymore," joked Richards.

"Hi, everybody!" said John. Julian knew him. And wouldn't have wished him on anyone. A nerd nightmare.

"Wayne Hill, Richie. What's the deal?" asked Chief Edwards.

Richards laughed heartily—the laugh made the speaker crackle annoyingly. "Boy, I don't envy you," said Richards, still chuckling. "The hands, huh? How 'bout the hand bit? How he studies 'em?"

"Yeah, the hands."

"How's your supply of fresh cranberries?" Richards laughed.

"Listen, Richie," said Edwards, not feeling so humorous, "any idea how he lost that finger?"

"Nope, never asked, never said. Tell you the truth, guy's so strange, I was afraid to bring it up. Hey, wanna get him riled? Take out a Polaroid and aim it at him."

"I don't understand it," said Edwards. "He won't allow a photograph, but he gobbles up the press."

"In fact, I think I've got the only known photo of him," Richards remarked. "Press clippin' when he solved the Pike Twin murders. Shows the whole team of us. You 'member that case, right? God, I look awful. I'll send you a copy, what the hell, you'll get a laugh."

"But what about it, Richie, is he for real?"

Richards turned suddenly sober. "Best I ever saw."

Edwards and Julian looked at each other.

"You know I've tried using a number of these guys—and gals, of course," he added deferentially, "over the years. Hell, I'll take it wherever I can get it. I ain't proud. Now, on that Pike case we was nowhere. Stalled for months. But this guy Hill comes in, feels up some of the items, the photos, took him to the scene, met the relations, and in four days he's got it. And I mean *got it*. Separate, corroborating confessions, corroborating evidence— it's a lock."

"What about the next one? The Church Bell case."

"Same. I would a put him on staff at that point."

"And the third one?"

"Nothin'. Zip. 'Ventually held up those crazy hands and shrugged his shoulders and said, 'Sorry.' "

"And that's about when he checked himself into Zimmern State?" said Edwards.

"Far as I know."

"You ever talk to his doctor?"

"The good Doc called me once, to verify some damn thing or other. Tibor? Was that it? Yeah. Dr. Tibor, I think."

"Yeah," said Edwards, "that's what he said."

"Look," said Richards, "I know he's a pain in the ass, I know he's an awful strange duck, but he solved those first two, and I mean *hisself*. Two out of three. That wins in this game, far as I'm concerned, don't it? What can I tell you? Hang in there. If he feels it, and he says he feels it, then odds are, 'ventually he'll get you somewhere."

"Let me ask you something," said Edwards. "Ever occur to you, ever strike you, that Wayne Hill himself might have committed that third murder?"

"Sure," said Richards cheerfully. "But there was never the least bit of evidence."

"That doesn't mean he didn't do it," said Edwards.

"Doesn't mean he did," countered Richards winsomely.

"Well—" Edwards looked sulky. "Thanks, Richie."

The next call was of course to Zimmern State.

Edwards kept it on the speakerphone.

"This is Chief Edwards, Canaanville Police. Is Dr. Tibor there, please?"

"Dr. Tibor is on vacation."

"Vacation!" The word exploded out of him. "How long?"

"A month in the Bahamas," said the nurse, openly envious.

"A month!"

"Psychiatrists," she said. "They take a month."

"I thought that's August."

"Hey, it's nice up here in August. So he goes

now, when it's already turned cold. Makes a lot more sense. But he'll be back in another week."

"Is there a number where he can be reached?"

"I'm sorry. No number."

"This is a police matter. I have to reach him."

"If you knew the kind of people Dr. Tibor sees all day, you wouldn't leave a number, either," the nurse confided. "Maybe I can help you?"

"I doubt it. I need information on a patient of his, Wayne Hill."

"You know I can't give you that."

"I *know*. That's why I need Tibor."

"Sorry."

"Well, look, I mean, is Mr. Hill currently in treatment? Tell me that, at least."

She breathed. "Now, Chief, you know this kind of thing is confidential information. But okay, yes he is. He sees Dr. Tibor three times a week. Of course, not right now, while the doctor's on vacation."

"And can you just tell me—"

"Sorry," the nurse cut him off. "You'd have to talk to Tibor himself."

"Thank you."

He jabbed the squawkbox button angrily to shut it off.

"The Bahamas. A month. Must be nice."

SIXTEEN

Julian brought her three bulging bags over to the Edwards home that evening. Estelle finally had prevailed. She simply could not bear to have that young lady in that Ramada one more minute.

As for Julian, faced with living with Wayne at the Ramada—with his strange nocturnal roamings, leering smile, and raspy voice—or living with the Chief and his wife, in an immaculate house of calm smiles and corkscrewing tension, the choice wasn't much of one. Canaanville was indeed small. Small enough, she knew, that Estelle's offer to her would somehow become generally known. To decline would be an affront to basic hospitability—maybe the plainest, gravest affront there was in a small town. How could she insult the wife of the chief of police like that? Eventually she accepted the Edwardses' offer.

Her choice was somewhat vindicated when she saw the apartment over the barn. Charming, homey, exposed beams, a wood-burning stove, big picture windows looking out onto the woods . . . its own entrance—albeit up a flight of wooden steps. "No phone, I'm afraid," said Edwards. "Took it out when the kids left, but fireplace has a good draw, and well . . ." He waved a hand toward the rest of the apartment, vaguely indicating its virtues.

At the end of the perfunctory apartment tour, Edwards regarded Julian with a kind of frank glumness. "The Missus insists you join us for dinner. First-night welcome." His clipped, formal delivery of the invitation indicated he did not wish to discuss it—or anything else—any further right now.

She simply smiled at the Chief.

Dinner. Oh goody. Starting right in.

"I just couldn't have you down there in that Ramada another night," said Estelle Edwards, carting steaming dish after steaming dish into the tiny, surprisingly elegant Victorian dining room. "And it'll be good to have another voice around the house, what with all the kids gone. And if I can't trust this one after thirty years . . ." joked Estelle, gesturing toward the Chief, and she let the rest of the thought slide as understood.

Heaping portions of steaming pot roast, peeled Maine potatoes, and mixed vegetables on unadorned china . . . *It doesn't come any more American than this,* thought Julian. "Go to," said Mrs. Edwards, and Julian hoped the woman did not harbor the secret agenda of "fattening her up."

And between the steaming helpings, the clatter of china and silver, the satisfying gulps of cider, and the equally glittering and sharp-sounding clattering chatter of Estelle Edwards, Julian soon enough gathered the story of Winston and Estelle. Their courtship the first year Winston was assigned to Canaanville. Of the dairy farm nearby that was still in Estelle's family. Of the beautiful day she and Edwards were married, the Edwards clan mysterious and diffident compared to her own—and *dairy farmers* were supposed to be laconic. "Do you know, Winston's mother came up to me that day, seemed to look right above my head somewhere, told me we'd have three children, and then just walked away. And lo and behold. Three children. I'll never forget that."

Edwards grunted.

She rambled on about son Michael's medical internships, and son Peter's first years in practice and first courtroom appearances, and daughter Stephanie's studies and papers, and while a mother's pride normally might be cockle-warming to see, somehow Estelle's bluster was trying to prove something, to summon and assure self-worth out of her children's accomplishments. It was somehow a plea, a begging, for her own worthiness, so that every word was grating, challenging. What was she trying to prove? What was she so stridently trying to say? Or to cover up? The inchoate detective detected something.

"And what about you, Julian?"

Estelle's sudden question, the sudden cessation of her own relentless monologue, caught Julian off guard. Julian looked at her, alarmed, alert. Estelle smiled warmly. "What can you tell us about *you*?"

Clearly—it would seem—Edwards didn't speak much to his wife. For if Edwards *had* said anything, Julian was sure, Estelle never would have asked the question so innocently and blithely. Julian was startled to discover this degree of distance in a marriage of thirty years. He'd never said *anything* about his new young assistant? Where she came from, her history? There must have been at least *some* curiosity on Estelle's part. Or perhaps nothing had been said simply because, here in the country, it was distastefully considered gossip. Though Julian could not help but sense the tenor of it fully, with clarity: Not much life got passed between Winston and Estelle Edwards. In their immaculate little Victorian home together, they inhabited separate universes.

And how could she answer, really, at this pleasant little get-together, this nice civil dinner? *Oh, well, my daddy was killed in the next room while I listened from my bed. My family never recovered, and I've been on my own since the day I could thumb a ride.*

She thought of the resumé. The impressive resumé she had brought Edwards that first day. Its orderly, illustrious line of perfect 4.0's and A's and dutiful work in soup kitchens and cancer wards. The work-study program to finish high school, the hard-won scholarships to the Academy, the night-shift waitressing and clerical jobs till three and four in the morning, just to scrape by. Her stunning Academy ranking. No one had ever thought to ask the most obvious question, looking at all that: *Why?* Funny they hadn't asked. She could answer. She knew why. *Because I can only bear to live on that highly organized sheet of paper. Only know how to live on the order of that page, and no longer in the confusion of real life, in the chaos of actual wants and needs. I will do what's right, I will perform perfectly, because I have no idea what else to do, I have no idea who I am, what I want, beyond the return of what I had before the disaster.*

*If I can't have that—and I can't—then I have no
notion of what to do. And I'll do whatever will look
best. You see, I'm absent. Mark me absent. Absent
from life. Shut down. So just tell me what to do,
and I'll do it.*

"So what about you, dear?" Estelle asked again
gently.

"Oh, well, you know . . ." Demurely. *Save me,
Winston. Say something.* But Edwards sat chewing,
eyes studiously to his plate. "Not much to tell, really," Julian began. "Little town in the South. Col-
lege in the big city . . ."

"The South! Why, I'd have never known! No
accent at all! I was down south just once, in New
Orleans. Tell you what I loved about that city . . ."
And she was off and running again.

Julian didn't know how she would bear all the
dinners to come, since she was proving such an
adept listener, if a poor conversationalist.

Shifting in her chair, she swung her toe under
the table, and found a foot.

An accident.

Edwards looked up suddenly over his bifocals,
and she knew whose foot she had found.

She let her foot dangle a moment, as if on a
precipice, a ledge of some kind—judging, debat-
ing, undecided.

The evening in North Carolina had continued

to play on her mind, ceaselessly, inescapably, complex. Clearly she had witnessed something. Something simmering in him, searching for release, in that odd, too-intense moment in the hallway. But the full reality of that moment was shaded, subtly textured. Because something, after all, had been simmering in her, too.

Absent. Mark me absent. Her sexual life, with a chaste handful of partners, had been competent, functional, and utterly without genuine feeling. *Absent. Mark me absent. Tell me what you want me to do, and I'll do it.* She had always assumed that that night, the snidely laughing sheriff's men, her entire, strange life, had taken a certain capacity of feeling out of her, absented it. But then, up here, unexpectedly, with eccentric, irascible, ugly, and amazing Edwards across the scarred desk, across the candlelit dinner table in North Carolina, at the ice machine outside her hotel door, a feeling had materialized. A feeling of attraction so alien it had been a shock to her, to feel something like that.

The wrongness of it had hit her bluntly. Though the wrongness of it, for all she knew, was part of it. She was, after all, inexperienced with attraction, was the first to admit it.

And there she had been in the hallway, undecided, mixed feelings, immersed in a hopelessly incomprehensible swirl of excitement, guilt, embarrassment, curiosity. Incomprehensible, that is, to someone absent from any like feeling before.

And then—as if to mock the awakening of the feeling—she had seen whatever it was in Edwards' eyes. Pulsing in his jaw. Crushing her fingers . . .

Something—in her chaste handful of previous partners—she had never seen before.

Her sexual experience was limited. Admittedly, she didn't know much. But she knew enough to be frightened.

Quietly, to the accompaniment of Estelle's continuing babble and plate-heaping, Julian slipped off her shoe.

It was wrong.

She knew how wrong.

Now she touched—barely touched—the Chief's ankle with her toe.

The fear rushed through her: vague, real.

The Chief, eating studiously, couldn't help but allow a little smile to pass between bites.

Wrong. A mistake.

She knew how wrong.

She felt the fear.

But there was something Winston Edwards wasn't saying. Not with words, anyway. But something his lumbering presence had whispered to her out in that hallway in North Carolina. Something in his expression, in the bear-paw squeeze of her hand, something she had felt beneath the sheer nightshirt, felt along her tanned skin, something she had sensed in her bones.

There was some truth Edwards was hiding. She could feel it.

And the chance of getting to it somehow, she knew, was the real reason she had accepted the Edwardses' offer.

And if it took a literal, physical stripping to the truth to find it, where was it written that was wrong? Wouldn't that demonstrate the true mark, the full commitment, the utter soul, of a detective? A more complete detective than the Academy might recommend—but who would have to know except her?

In the circling of her toe beneath the table, she circled the possibility.

Self-destructive? Some deep, previously un-tapped self-destructive streak? All her life, she had observed the self-destructive behavior of others. Girlfriends. Male friends. The hard-luck cases of her Academy casework. How they repeated, re-lived, replayed, some original disaster. To experi-ence its life-altering power again? To try somehow to change it? Guilt at having survived it? Was she unwittingly entering the zone where she'd seen so many go before?

Or was her quest for the truth a convenient

story she was telling herself, a little girl's pink lie, to make more acceptable, more palatable, the urge to sleep with a man old enough to be her father?

But he was *not* her father.

She withdrew her toe.

She saw the smile fade.

And only now did she experience, at last, a genuine sense of threat. Its clarity, its hard lines, caught her by surprise. Threat, wafting up with its own rich and cloying scent from the Edwardses' dinner table. Some observing part of her, separate but clear, semaphoring warning, waving the flags wildly . . .

Wrong. A mistake.

She felt the fear.

She felt the rush.

Life had cut her off. Set her adrift. And here somehow, in Winston Edwards, there was a lifeline. But how, exactly, should she grab it? With both hands, kicking wildly, before you go under again? Or test the rope first, with one hand only?

Keeping your other hand and legs free to swim with.

Should the need arise.

SEVENTEEN

In moonlight somehow blindingly bright, shimmering with portent in its reflections in the stream, Sarah Langley's severed arms batted him mercilessly, repeatedly—*thud! thwack! thud!*—on the back . . . the neck . . . the ears . . . Her head, spewing blood explosively, flew like a ball at Winston Edwards in the marsh.

Duck! Duck!

He sat bolt upright, breathless, at two A.M. . . .

He waited in the dark, to hear his breath catch its measure.

He looked to his side.

Estelle snored undisturbed.

Winston lay in bed, thinking about the murder of Sarah Langley.

It was what he usually did, awakened from one

of the nightmares. It was how he had solved a couple of cases, in fact.

But tonight, it was different.

Tonight he could not get back to sleep.

Because tonight, Julian Palmer was in the barn two hundred yards down the path.

The deep, snapping cold of the November night hung wolflike outside the barn apartment, frosting the windows as if with bitter breath, howling at her in wind like a madman's incessant, rhythmic but strangely tuneful wail and hum. The wind in gusts swirled around the barn in a fierce dance, a song of night angry and alive. The silence after each gust, a lull, that commanded rapt attention.

She lay on the bed, staring at the ceiling, listening to the howling of the wind. . . .

Feeling again, the huge palm on her stomach. The grazing dance of ankle and toe beneath the table.

Trying to sort flirtation from intention. . . .

Wondering, vaguely, if she'd hear, within that howling wind, a knock on the barn apartment door. . . .

Or if the signals were still as mixed to him as they were to herself.

His incredible instincts. Probably he could read the blur of her own feelings. . . .

Two hundred yards down the path from Winston Edwards, Julian Palmer could not sleep, either.

In the kitchen, restless, Winston rattles around.

He looks at the knife rack.

All the knives are there.

EIGHTEEN

Art, the reporter from the *Albany Mail*, stood on the station-house steps, jumping against the morning cold, breath-clouds rising thickly, and chatting amiably—too amiably—with Wayne Hill.

"Here again, Art?" Julian asked, coming up the steps herself. "You know what the Chief said," she warned sternly, watching her own breath rise to join theirs.

"Well, little Miz Palmer, doin' the Chief's bidding," said Art, in a taunting greeting. "How far you go in doing his bidding, Miz Palmer?"

Julian glared at Hill.

White-hot rage surged through her, a jolt. She did her best to contain it.

"You get back to the Ramada," she said to Hill, "and you wait there till we send for you."

"Gee, a junior Winston Edwards," said Art under his breath as Julian walked away.

She whirled to face him, and glowered. But what could she do?

As she did every morning, she began by opening Edwards' mail.

The astonishing number of legal communications, lab reports, briefings, continued unabated.

The amount of paperwork in police work was sobering.

Through the partition, she could see Edwards hunched over his own desk as she worked.

Suddenly Julian had reason to smile.

There was a manila envelope with a City of Northward return address. Chief Richards' jurisdiction. It was the article on Wayne Hill that Chief Richards had promised to send.

She opened the envelope, unfolded the article.

The photograph was surprisingly clear for a photocopy of an old newspaper clipping. *Syracuse Times*. July 30, 1982. LOCAL PSYCHIC HELPS CATCH KILLER, the headline proclaimed with an amusing touch of civic pride.

She looked at the photograph. Wayne Hill wasn't in it.

Obviously Richards had sent down the wrong

article. On the phone, his whole operation had sounded a little lax and loose to Julian anyway. She snickered and put the article aside. As it landed on the pile on her desk, she read the caption beneath the photo:

> Standing at the crime scene, left to right, Chief Richards of the Northward Police, Sergeant Stuart Mickel, local psychic Wayne Hill, County First Selectman Otto Ferlinger . . .

But that *wasn't* Wayne Hill. It was someone else. . . .

Tall, stooped, balding . . .

She held the photograph close to the desk lamp.

The man was missing a little finger.

What on earth . . . ?

Very quickly it dawned on her.

Her guts reported it, and her rational mind followed close behind.

The man in the photograph in front of her was indeed Wayne Hill.

And the man they had been working with this eventful past week was not.

In disbelief, she began to read:

Wayne Hill, a local psychic, virtually sin-
glehandedly solved the Pike Twin murder
case that has plagued the Northward Police
Department for months. . . .

She couldn't continue. She couldn't concentrate.

She and Edwards had never asked Hill for
identification. Why would they? They'd had his
quirks and methods described in detail by Richards
and others over the phone, and it was so obviously
him. But they'd never, after all, seen the single
known photograph of him.

And now she had.

She scooped up the article and breezed quickly into
Chief Edwards' office.

He looked up slowly at her, then suddenly
cocked his huge, ursine head to an angle of alertness, as if sensing something even from the manner
of her entrance.

"I'm glad you're sitting," she said.

She shoved the article in front of him.

She thought she had seen him angry before.

She saw now that those times had only been a
dry run. A dress rehearsal.

And Julian knew—finally knew—knew in her
bones, that they were dealing with a killer.

NINETEEN

Wayne Hill—or whoever he really was—sat in the Chief's office, prepared to continue, unaware of what Julian and Edwards had discovered.

The station-house floor was empty. Eerie. As if a bomb had dropped.

Or was about to.

"Okay, Wayne," said Edwards, sitting up, playing the role, "the files are outside this office, the floor is cleared of personnel, just as you asked. Let's make today really count," said Edwards.

Control yourself, Chief, don't blow it, thought Julian.

"Let's see if we can really make something happen today."

Don't blow it, Winston, don't lose your cool. . . .

"Oh, Chief Edwards," said Hill, oblivious, unsuspecting, "I wish it were all so simple. . . ."

*   *   *

Hill turned now to Julian: "Okay, begin to bring the files closer," he commanded.

Following Hill's previous instruction, Julian walked the first set of files closer, one step at a time.

The strange emptiness of the station house, the meticulous movement of just one body within it, the silence . . .

"Stop!" commanded Hill.

Julian stopped.

Wayne Hill looked, as if startled, down at his hands.

"I'm getting . . . again . . . this—I don't know, a counterwave, something wrong. . . . *No,*" he said suddenly, the "no" punched out of him. "A jade necklace . . ."

The necklace again, thought Julian. *This necklace that was never found. What is this necklace?*

"It's like. Like . . ." Wayne Hill looked up, right at Julian, but seemed not to see her, to look right through her at something mesmerizing, something terrifying. "Like he's *still killing her,*" he said, confused, and looked down at his hands again.

"Who are you? Who the hell are you?" the Chief said suddenly.

Too fast, she thought. *Too fast. . . .*

But Wayne Hill seemed to not hear Edwards, as he concentrated powerfully on his own hands. . . .

"He's . . . he's still with her," said Wayne Hill.

"This is impossible!" Edwards bellowed, rising from behind his desk—pure force, pure threat, gathering. . . .

"Wait, please. I'm . . . I'm getting something. At last. Something!"

The hand with the missing finger now danced in front of them. "Jesus," Hill said, "it's . . . *here.*"

The hand shook, as if palsied. "It's . . . I can almost . . . It's . . . Oh my God, no wonder I couldn't—no wonder! . . . *The crime isn't over yet! The killer is still with the girl!*"

What kind of nonsense, thought Julian . . .

Edwards came around the desk. "This has gone far enough!"

"In your wallet, Chief! He's with the girl in your wallet!"

What the . . . ?

Hill's head shuddered in an involuntary spasm. "The *name!*" His eyes widened—frightened, stunned, triumphant. *"The name is all over your wallet!"*

Edwards rose. "This is ridiculous! You couldn't . . ."

"Where you still have her, don't you?" said Wayne Hill, looking up from his hands, no longer shaking, and straight into the Chief's eyes. "Where you're still together, aren't you?"

The photograph, thought Julian. *The high-school photo in Edwards' wallet.*

"You're not a psychic!" screamed Winston Edwards. "You couldn't know! Only I could . . ."

"I couldn't know?" said Wayne Hill. "Only you could know? And why is that, Winston?" Wayne Hill's raspy voice was suddenly gone, replaced by one that was conventional but firm. Wayne Hill—or whoever he was—turned to Julian in a way she never had seen in the past week, a way suddenly self-possessed, assured. "Use your deductive powers, Miss Palmer. Use what they taught you." He turned back to Edwards. "Why could only you know?"

"That's a figure of—"

"Only you could know? I couldn't know? Why is that? Because I wasn't there, after all? And you were?"

"You're not a psychic!" Winston Edwards raged.

"No, I'm not," the man quietly agreed.

"Then what the hell *are* you?"

"A witness."

And through the confusion and the blurred

meanings and the possibilities that seemed to spiral around Winston Edwards' suddenly unfamiliar office, Julian could process only the two words: *a witness.*

She saw the huge fists, the huge bear-paws clench. . . . The Chief straightened, fuming. She had never seen such rage. His veins bulged. His jaw locked. "Impossible. You weren't there! I just *know* you weren't—"

What was happening here? But Julian's instincts—those trustworthy/untrustworthy instincts—were telling her what indeed was happening here, and she felt steadily dizzier.

No wonder the investigation had stalled.

Those pictures, those glossy pictures—severed head, ribboned torso, missing lips and nose—splayed across his walls. . . .

"*. . . police presence. I'm getting . . . a police presence . . .*"

The floor was still empty, but felt crowded, flooded, jammed, and confused. . . .

Edwards looked now at Julian.

She looked back at him, expressionlessly.

Wayne Hill turned to her as well.

There was a thick silence. A silence filled to bursting.

Jesus Christ, she thought.

What do I do? What do I do?

Edwards looked a long time at her. Then, in a suddenly reserved, formal voice, he broke the silence. "I'm going to make a phone call," Edwards said. "I get to make a phone call, don't I?" he added, smiling ruefully.

Oh my God. Is it true?

Julian couldn't speak. She barely managed to stand.

Chief Edwards. Winston Edwards. The Bear . . .

A nausea rose up slowly but inexorably in her like a tide, washing over any other feeling or thought in her . . .

"Maybe you'd better give Julian the picture first," said the man.

Winston Edwards reached for his wallet in his rear pocket, took out the high-school photograph of Sarah Langley that he carried with him, looked at it quickly once more, and handed it wordlessly to the man, who in turn handed it to Julian—who took it, shaking.

"Evidence," the man said quietly.

TWENTY

As Julian watched Edwards on the phone in a small, empty office beyond the familiar glass partition, the man sat down heavily, exhausted but triumphant, into Winston Edwards' scarred and ancient chair, and told her the astonishing story.

Julian's revulsion came now in relentless, steady waves. Her clarity, her reason, her analytic skills, seemed useless, tossed aside, in oceanic events.

Their evening in Raleigh-Durham, their intimate conversations, the hallway encounter, the touching of feet under the table—replayed in an endless loop, inescapable, tyrannical, the brain's own clever torture, and it was all she could do to concentrate, to listen to the man's astounding tale. Fortunately, it was astounding enough to battle the waves of Julian's revulsion.

His name was Dr. Tibor.

My God, she thought. *Dr. Tibor. Wayne Hill's psychiatrist.*

And clearly he was not having the Bahamas vacation his nurse had imagined.

"I've treated Mr. Hill, in fact, for years, so miming his mannerisms, his quirks, his voice, was easy. And his aversion to photographs worked, of course, in my favor. Could I . . . could I get a cup of water?" He smiled weakly. "No more fresh cranberries."

Dr. Tibor. Wayne Hill's psychiatrist. The *real* Wayne Hill's psychiatrist. Julian felt unsteady, reorienting herself as she listened. He took a sip of the water she handed him, and dutifully continued. "I met Sarah Langley on a camping trip last year." He sipped the water again, then looked up at Julian, and waited a moment, to let the significance of this statement begin to sink in. "The affair began immediately," he said with formality. "And that night I was coming to see her, rounding the corner of her block, when I saw her being dragged outside and into a sedan with what looked like official plates, I was too far away to be sure. I ran to catch up, to see what on earth was going on, but they had pulled out quickly and were down the block in no time.

"And then quite suddenly, the car stopped there at the end of the block, and I saw a hulking figure half push and half carry Sarah into the park. I would have yelled, but I soon saw who the figure was. I recognized him from newspaper articles. The famous Chief. Winston Edwards."

A fresh wave of revulsion rose up in Julian, gnawed at her insides, challenged her balance. "Please continue," she said.

Please don't, she thought. . . .

"Well, I followed them." A beat. An involuntary shiver. "What happened next was, well . . ."

He ceased talking quite suddenly, looked down—this time, she noticed, not at his hands at all.

He looked up, imploringly. "I realized it would all come down to my word against his. The word of a shrink, a weirdo head-doctor, against that of a respected and feared police chief. What power did I have?" He gulped the water now. "Well, the power of my profession. The power of my own training. Human nature. My only chance." He smiled palely. "I knew no man could live with the guilt of having done what I saw Edwards do. The nightmares would be continual. And that's where the plan for the impersonation came from. To elicit the guilt, tease it out, the guilt that had to be there."

So this was how the doctor had chosen to spend his vacation. Not on some pristine beach in the Bahamas as his staff had thought. But Julian took it in absently, for her attention had focused now on something else. "The finger. . . . You . . . you cut off your finger?!"

"I loved her," said Dr. Tibor, in a simple and complete explanation, looking up at Julian again. "I should have saved her then, somehow. And I'm trying—trying now—to redeem that moment of failure."

Sacrifice, guilt, heroism—the full extent of Dr. Tibor's story, of Dr. Tibor's existence these past few weeks, began slowly to expand now in Julian's mind, to obtrude where her own sordid preoccupations had previously consumed it.

"So your talking to the *Albany Mail*, and the new white suit you bought . . ."

"That's all Wayne Hill," said Tibor. "Believe me. Irascible. Difficult. Egotistical. I had to make it convincing."

"But how . . ." Julian was racing now to piece it all together, and as she did so she saw that everything fit, fell into place. "How did you know about the photograph in Edwards' wallet?"

Tibor smiled. "When we headed out to inspect Sarah's apartment, I saw Edwards take it out and look at it with you, through the glass partition." He gulped. "Sarah's apartment." His Adam's apple bobbed. He paused—then pushed on, dutifully continued, a foot soldier to the telling. "I couldn't actually see who was in the photograph, but it was pretty obvious who it must be. All that stuff about 'a police presence' and 'something blocking me,' I started all that once I knew the picture was in his wallet. Once I knew about that picture, I knew I had my final moment."

Tibor must indeed have loved her, truly loved her. What opposition, what stark contrast, to what Julian now felt about the huge and gruesome figure dialing fervently in the next office. Her revulsion rose up again—threatening her balance—stronger, stronger. . . .

She never had seen a man so thoroughly exhausted. Tibor could hardly keep his eyes open. It seemed he couldn't lift his arms, move his legs. He seemed to have deflated, evaporated, to not be there. But the stunt was over. It had ended. He breathed a sigh.

"Oh," he suddenly said—and with some last reserve of energy, he reached deep into his pocket and took out a necklace made of jade. "I gave it to her the month I met her. Edwards knew he'd seen it. It fell from Sarah's neck in the park. I picked it up." He ha   d it gingerly, affectionately, sorrowfully, to Julian Palmer. "More evidence," he said quietly. Julian looked at him. His eyes were filled with tears.

In those years when Julian had sought her escape in the city, sought to eradicate her past in its noisy, teeming brightness, the city had cooperated infinitely, offering solace in various forms: in its sheer size and the sheer numbers of its humanity, to feel gloriously hidden within of course; but also in its entertainments, its diversions; its all-night movie houses, its tabloid dramas; and in her neighbor's arguments, in her roommates' romantic escapades, in the variously engaging, entertaining, inevitably lighter pasts of others. But they were all stories, after all, each a drama unto itself. Twisting, tangled stories, stories—best of all—not her own. And the tangle of those stories—on the screen, in the morning edition, from the soul of an apartment-mate sunk deep in a broken-spined Salvation Army couch at three in the morning—stories imaginary and real and not her own, often had succeeded in diverting her.

But here she was, back in a small town, on a murder investigation; inevitably, a mirror of the bitter reality she had sought to escape long ago. A mirror she had expected, been prepared for—a return to the pain, to the raw awareness of it and, she hoped, to a "solving" of some sort. Here she was, in a return to a small town, and already it was more compelling than anything the city had proffered.

What that must have taken, to impersonate Hill like that. Each night in the Ramada, spent planning, rehearsing, thinking through. Each day in contact with Edwards and Julian, measuring every movement. Considering each word. The control. The patience. Wearing a shell. Wearing another life.

Wearing another life. She knew exactly what it took. She was a kind of impersonator too. Impersonating confidence. Impersonating happiness. Substituting no past for a brutalizing one.

The few possible witnesses, the few possible suspects, gone now. Gone for some time. Passed away peacefully, rocking on their front porches, or in their daybeds, looking out on favorite maple trees, surrounding by progeny. All the relevant papers were relevant no more, rubber-banded together in a file case deep in the ramshackle police station. Her father's murder. Unsolved. Still trying to accept it. Unsolved forever.

It was an astonishing story Tibor told. It was the most astonishing story Julian had ever heard.

It was about to get more so.

Chief Edwards, visible in the small neighboring office through the glass partition, hung up the phone, and came back into his own office.

What am I going to do, arrest him? she thought. *Arrest Winston Edwards?* Julian turned the moment over frantically, trying to master it.

Edwards smiled ruefully at Dr. Tibor—his adversary, his nemesis, his downfall.

"This is Dr. Tibor," said Julian Palmer to Winston Edwards . . . as introduction, explanation, unable to think of anything else to say, and with the vague notion that perhaps even now the good Doctor could somehow begin to help Chief Edwards.

"No it's not," smiled Winston Edwards.

What?

"See, I just got off the phone with Dr. Tibor," said Edwards, "who is just back from the Bahamas—suntanned, I'm sure—sounding perfectly relaxed. Our conversation quickly found its way past his patient Wayne Hill to another longtime patient of his, one in the habit of reading other patients' files, in the habit of petty crimes, a series of them for which he is at the hospital, in fact. A patient who as it happens missed his appointment today, has been missing all of them recently, and who did not have an appointment with Dr. Tibor on the day Sarah Langley was killed. Eugene Green is that patient's name. Small-time thief, amateur psychiatrist." Edwards looked at the man. "Hello, Mr. Green."

"Hello, Chief Edwards," said the man.

Beneath her conservative skirt and blouse, Julian felt herself shaking.

"I'm glad you've made yourself comfortable here over the past week, Mr. Green, because you're going to be here awhile. And you'll be missing a few more appointments with Dr. Tibor. Because you're now under arrest for the murder of Sarah Langley."

TWENTY-ONE

"You couldn't know!"

"You weren't there!"

The words, the phrases, the raging counter-assertions, uttered by Winston "Bear" Edwards at the moment when the Great Chief had been suddenly accused.

Words, phrases, uttered at the moment of shock and surprise, when they had the least chance of being monitored, or coached, or of dancing adeptly to one side or another, dodging the ray of truth.

The words came back to her now, perfectly accurately, perfectly recalled in her viselike memory.

You weren't there. You couldn't know. . . .

Words and phrases so perfectly poised, so perfectly balanced, between two meanings.

"You weren't there. You couldn't know." She said the words aloud, but the meaning stayed balanced on the tightrope of her consciousness, as she lay there in the dark, staring at the outline of the barn bedroom's exposed beams in the dim moonlight.

The fragments rushed at her. . . .

"Maybe he found it . . . I don't know . . . alluring," he'd said of Wayne Hill and murder at dinner that night in Raleigh-Durham. *"Maybe it swept him up somehow . . . and maybe the feeling was . . . well, intoxicating."* Speculations in the candlelight. Or was it, with momentary benefit of candlelight and alcohol, a confession-in-passing, a slightly dropped guard? Had the moment even been about Wayne Hill at all?

And at that dinner, why had he still entertained—no, clung to the idea, that Wayne Hill was perhaps truly psychic? Because he *knew* Hill hadn't killed Sarah Langley? So Hill couldn't know the clues *except* as a psychic?

Knowing where the drinking glasses were—the strange little cabinet—in Sarah Langley's apartment. Edwards could have remembered from earlier inspections of the place. He was thorough, obsessive, after all. He could have remembered from an earlier inspection, couldn't he?

Knowing to lift the bathroom door to make it

latch. He could have discovered that on a previous visit. He could have. Couldn't he?

And his not shutting the bathroom door. Which anyone might do out of easy habit, in a lover's apartment.

"It's always surprised me there isn't more violent crime in this park . . . such a perfect place," he'd commented that day in Veterans' Park. *"Because nobody in Southside thinks to hide anything."* Meaning that Winston Edwards does? *"Such a perfect place. . . ."*

"People around here ain't generally all that bright," he'd said that first morning of work.

Meaning he could get away with it?

Julian Palmer lay in bed, staring at the exposed beams, and contemplated the impossible prospect.

That Winston Edwards had killed Sarah Langley.

Then why would he have taken on a psychic?

Unfortunately, there were some very good reasons.

It had struck her as oddly noble—even before she knew him better—when Edwards himself had said that it might be construed as obstruction of justice, or impeding an investigation, not to follow through every possibility. But now such over-diligence made sense. If Edwards *had* committed the crime, then he certainly needed to appear to be taking every possible measure in trying to solve it.

But more than that, there was a steadily growing community pressure, to say nothing of the pre-existing pressure of a long and legendary career of successful criminal investigation—to at least offer the appearance of exhausting all possible avenues in trying to solve the crime.

"*How would it look if I didn't chase down every possibility?*" he had said.

"*And have you ever had any luck with any of these guys?*" she'd asked him.

"*No,*" he'd smiled. Figuring, no doubt, he was safe.

But then the "psychic" had provided a couple of clues, and begun to brag to the press, and then Edwards couldn't very well get rid of him, particularly since Julian, his new young assistant, now knew of the clues too.

It occurred to her that Edwards may have agreed to hiring *her* simply to have someone to show, and to prove, that he was doing a thorough investigative job.

But when the psychic's clues proved disconcertingly accurate, a little more than psychic—more likely those of some sort of witness—Edwards couldn't very well eliminate him. How would he, anyway? Commit another murder? So he had to keep Hill on at that point, to play it out, to see what was going on. . . .

"So you start to wonder—to see how—there could be a Perfect Crime," he had said that second day, seemingly in abject, powerless desperation.

It looked now like he meant it in malicious triumph.

A Perfect Crime. His use of the ridiculous phrase came back to her now. Because when Eugene Green had happened along, and posing as Wayne Hill had begun revealing valid clue after valid clue, Edwards the murderer may have seen not only the threat to him, but also, ironically, the possibility: of making a Perfect Crime even more perfect.

That is, instead of leaving the crime unsolved, *finding the murderer*—someone who clearly, by his behavior, by his steadily revealed knowledge, would appear to have committed the crime.

The evolution of a Perfect Crime to an Even More Perfect Crime.

Julian had noticed that Edwards insisted she be in on every phase of the investigation—calls on the speakerphone, visits to Southside, the walks to the crime scene, the trip to Raleigh-Durham . . .

But she noticed that Eugene Green had insisted on the same thing. Even when the office had been cleared out for Green's final Wayne Hill performance—for what Edwards and Julian knew would be a final confrontation—Green had specifically asked that Julian be there.

As if Green needed her as a witness, to corroborate his version of events.

As much as Chief Edwards needed her to believe his own. They both saw her as their best witness, it seemed. Both their corroborations, in trying to convince of the other's guilt.

She suddenly remembered something, got out of her bed, reached into her right suit pocket and fished out the jade necklace that "Tibor"—Green—had given her.

The necklace Edwards couldn't explain; but now, maybe, was simply refusing to.

Edwards hadn't seen Green give it to her. He'd been in the next office, making his phone call.

She wasn't sure why, but she was going to keep it awhile.

The wind swirled fiercely around the barn apartment.

Thoughts, images, scenarios, swirled fiercely around her mind.

With one possibility, one motivating, organizing suspicion, behind them all. . . .

That her fascinating employer, her mentor, her dining partner—a man toward whom she had felt some indistinguishable, complex mix of admiration, comfort, and attraction, was, additionally, an extremely clever cold-blooded killer, and sleeping two hundred yards away from her. . . .

That is, if he was sleeping at all.

She shifted uncomfortably in the bed.

What would she do? What *could* she do?

You weren't there.

You couldn't know.

But somehow she sensed—inevitably, inescapably, whether she wanted to or not—that she was going to.

Two hours later, she awakened to footsteps on the deck outside.

The deck creaking under the weight. . . .

Oh my God.

The footsteps scrabbling, moving quickly around in the moonlight. . . .

Get out of the line of sight. Instinctively she rolled off the bed, onto the floor.

Rolled to the wall. . . .

Worked her way toward the window. . . .

Held her breath.

Waited.

Silence.

No movement.

Nosing under the curtain, she looked cautiously, tentatively, out the window.

She sighed.

She smiled.

Then didn't.

The realization and the irony assaulted her together.

It was a bear.

A black bear, foraging. Its dark coat matted, imperfect, with the struggle of winter life.

Must have smelled something. The sweet smoke from the chimney, the scents tumbling from the warmth, the aromas of the trash . . .

Or simply, sensed life. The barn apartment, now occupied, after having been so long empty.

Maybe just the scent of *her*, Julian thought uncomfortably.

She watched, fascinated. Its lumbering, lazy investigative turns on the deck.

Until it turned its blank, black, amoral eyes toward her, staring, unhurried, only vaguely curious, through the window, at her.

A bear.

Fascinating to watch.

No doubt dangerous if cornered.

In a moment, it turned its eyes away again, as

thoughtlessly, as unconsidered, as it had turned them toward her. With an odd, feminine delicacy, it lumbered down the wooden steps, off into the woods.

Unknowable.

TWENTY-TWO

"Miz Palmer." He summoned her the next morning from her desk outside, at a volume anyone in the station house could hear. Boisterous, hearty, seemingly unaffected by the events of the day before. If anything, emboldened and invigorated by them.

She rose, and with dread, with doubt, with nervousness, entered his office to see him, to look at him, to sit with him, to work with him, for the first time since the startling circle of accusations.

"So," he said expansively, smiling genially at her as she took her customary seat.

"So," she said cautiously, guardedly, noncommittally back.

The deep wrinkles and pockmarks, the mottle of his weathered face—it all turned now to sinisterness, to fleshy trenches where villainy could hide. The brown limpid, liquid eyes—now hard marbles, unreadable, ungiving.

Instinctively, uncontrollably, she turned her eyes away.

Winston Edwards saw her do so; his head cocked attentively.

His mood shifted. He sighed deeply, shook his head, and hefted his huge, hulking frame out of the ancient leather chair.

He went over to the office door and closed it with uncharacteristic attention and care.

"Miz Palmer," he said again, far more gently this time. "I didn't know Sarah Langley." She heard the voice struggling for patience, a parent's exaggerated patience with a child. "Her picture was in my wallet because I wanted to find her killer. Same as the police photos on the wall. That's the way I've always worked. Ask Simms. Ask anyone. But ask, for Christ's sake"—the patience slipping slightly away from him now; and then, pausing to regain it, before continuing—"because I'm not going to be able to take your going over the line, with all your promise, with all your obvious, uh, assets. . . ." A slight, appraising smile.

Then suddenly turning away, and looking out the window, he added sourly, irritably, "Yes, I've had affairs. No, not with Sarah Langley. Discussion closed."

Flat, factual, assertive. Impressively plain and clear. And, heading back now to the familiar comfort of his ancient chair, "So let's get back to it, shall we?"

Expecting to continue, she saw, as if nothing had happened. As if everything was as it was before. As if to say clearly, implicitly, and unequivocally that good had triumphed and evil was behind bars, and nothing had changed. As if to seal and assure his version of events.

"Don't give out on me now," said Winston Edwards quietly, in another tone entirely—affectionate, gentle afterthought, smiling slightly and wryly, but beneath it, impatience and urgency, she sensed. "Don't go wiggy on me now." It was the voice of before, deliquescent, melting her.

Anticipating her questions, taking the offensive, clearing the air.

Admitting to some affairs—to explain his seeming comfort with the situation—but denying involvement with Sarah Langley.

Implying that her ruminations were sending her "over the edge"—the classic insulting male ploy. To reassure he was no more, no less, than the average, classic male.

Certainly not a killer. Couldn't be.

Clever. Smooth.

And behind her even now, Sarah Langley's

severed head and ribboned torso and brown-and-red scarred disks where her breasts had been, plastered on the glass-partition wall of Edwards' office, hanging there again.

Not a statistic. A real person.

The pictures glowed in her mind as never before—irrepressible, insistent.

It was all more than she had bargained for with the Associates Program.

A good bit more.

TWENTY-THREE

Lockup was unimproved since the building's construction in the 1930s. "No reason to update," Edwards had said gruffly on her opening-day tour. "We put about six guys a year down there, total, and anyway, works as a nice deterrent just the way it is."

It was dank and dark, considerably below street level, and more than a little medieval.

She descended into lockup to see Eugene Green.

It was the first thing she had done in open defiance of Winston Edwards. She suspected, somehow, it wouldn't be the last.

"Everything I said in his office was true," claimed Eugene Green, smiling wanly, "except, of course, for that minor detail about who I really am."

The cell was small, eight by eight, lit by a bare, dim bulb dead-center overhead. In the dim, strange light it cast, the ancient white sink and toilet gleamed eerily together in the far corner. He stood silent for a moment, then looked at her. "Would you have believed the story of a psychiatric hospital inmate who said he witnessed a murder? Would you believe his version of events, as opposed to a police chief's?"

The words bounced and bent and doubled back in the old vaults. "And you probably still don't believe me. But there's something about it, something in it, that holds you, that you *do* believe, something that strikes you about it, or you wouldn't be here, against Edwards' instructions, I'll bet."

And Julian was reminded again that Edwards' was not the only quick mind she was dealing with.

"How do you know Edwards doesn't want me here talking to you?" she asked.

"Because he knows I'm telling the truth," said Green. "And he doesn't want you to start to believe it." He regarded her challengingly.

"Dr. Tibor says you're an excellent liar."

"Well, that's no lie," smiled Eugene Green wickedly. "Who else but an excellent liar could have pulled off such an extended impersonation of the good doctor?"

There was arrogance there, arrogance and pride, she thought. Perhaps that was a way in, a way to a truth and reality that would convince her. A truth that was somewhere, somehow above Edwards' version of it or Green's version of it, a truth that had a ring of authenticity. That's what she was doing here, after all. That's why she had come down into the cold and dank. "Look," she began, trying to be natural, disarming, the fabled good cop, "you're clearly an extremely bright, intuitive man. . . ." But she saw immediately that it was a mistake. Eugene Green went suddenly rigid, fully alert to her ulterior motives. He seemed to know she was hoping to get somewhere with the compliment.

Then, slowly, like an urchin, he smiled. "Were you planning to try to trap me?" he asked, incredulous, on the verge of laughter. "Did you really think you could trap me?" he repeated, angrier now, accusatory, hostile. She saw in him now, for the first time, the hair-trigger emotions. Classic in the sociopath. "You'll never trap me," he said haughtily. "Never. For one very simple reason: I'm telling you the truth."

Julian sensed instantly that Eugene Green would see through anything that wasn't straightforward, and that in her own search for the truth, her own best trick might be truthfulness.

"Let's start from the beginning, then," she said. "How'd you meet Sarah?"

He smiled.

Better. Much better.

"Professionally," said Green.

"Meaning what?"

"Meaning she was a patient. Up there for help dealing with the deaths of her parents."

"Why all the way up to Zimmern State? Plenty of shrinks are plenty closer. Why go all the way up there?"

"Miss Palmer." He smiled. *He was going to lecture her. Just like Edwards.* It struck her. *Just like Edwards.* There was a forcefulness that was similar. An aggressively communicated wish to be left alone. A belligerent, bullying loneliness. "Canaanville, you've no doubt noticed, is an exceedingly small town. And she was, you've no doubt noticed, a lower-middle-class girl. Well, lower-middle-class girls are embarrassed to have anything to do with psychiatrists. Or have anyone know. She had to go that far away, to keep anyone from knowing."

"How long had you been seeing her?"

He shrugged. "I don't know. A year?"

"You don't know?" she said, and heard her own caustic tone too late.

"You listen to me," said Eugene Green, rising in his cell, his thin veneer of patience ripped away like tissue paper. "I loved her. You see this?" He held up his left hand, his missing finger. Julian took the opportunity, the invitation, to look long and directly at it for the first time. The fold of skin, pink on white, the ragged, discolored seam at the end of the scar. The freshness of it. "I *loved* her. I had to do *something*! He was going to get away with it! DO YOU UNDERSTAND THE NIGHT-MARE OF THAT?" The words echoed and bounced as if themselves tormented and impris-oned in the ancient brick and cinderblock.

In the long silence that followed, Julian shook her head, and looked up at him in incredulity, but in sympathy, too. "How did you ever think you'd get away with it?" she asked. "First being Hill. Then your psychiatrist?"

Eugene Green, as if directly in response to her moment of obviously honest sympathy, spoke with a sudden frankness and coherence and authority. Julian felt her own eyes widen slightly, as if to receive a full dose of the truth. "I knew Tibor was away. On vacation for the month. Enough time to pull it off. To ingratiate myself. To build it. Enough time for Edwards to crack. And I really thought he would. I *knew* he would. How could a sane man not?" he queried the dank corner of his cell again. "All that evidence, clue after clue. How could a sane man not?"

Eugene looked up at her. "How did I think I'd get away with it, Miss Palmer? Well, the point is, I almost did, didn't I?" he said quietly. Then looked down at his hands, his missing finger. "I almost did," he said again.

TWENTY-FOUR

Julian ascended the hard, cold stone steps, and was stopped just as hard and cold by a single thought.

"Deaths of her parents?" she said aloud.

Just now, Green had said Sarah came to Zimmern State looking for help dealing with the deaths of her parents. But Chief Edwards said Sarah's parents had visited him, and left the wallet photo.

Julian's heart pulsed.

Someone was lying.

The logbook! The logbook that Chief Edwards insisted every visitor sign.

Maybe it would finally prove as invaluable as Edwards had always claimed it was.

As she headed for the logbook, perched on its rickety wooden podium at the Canaanville station entrance, she realized excitedly that this was a chance—a first, perfect, clean chance—to weigh

Edwards' and Green's versions. Because in the matter of Sarah Langley's parents, at least, one of them had woven one corner of a tangled web. A web that maybe, at last, was beginning to tear.

"How far back does this sign-in book go?" she asked the desk clerk.

" 'Bout a year."

"Can I look through it?"

"That's why it's here."

Langley. Langley. Langley. She searched the book once, searched it again.

No entry by her parents.

It tended to confirm Eugene Green's point. Sarah's parents, it would seem from their absence from the logbook, were quite dead.

The dread rose in her again.

"What makes you think I saw her parents here in the station house?" said the Chief, his voice booming behind her an hour later.

She whirled, to see him facing her, his huge arms crossed.

Obviously the desk clerk had squawked. Trying to impress the Chief. She'd hoped the elderly clerk would simply forget about it, since he hadn't known what she was checking for. But the logbook was Edwards' baby, and dutifully, cowed, proud that his diligent keeping of the logbook was paying off in police work, the desk clerk obviously had reported its use to Edwards.

She was embarrassed. And furious.

"Would *you* have had the aggrieved parents come in here?" Edwards asked Julian sarcastically.

No, of course not. Which only occurred to Julian now. *But that's not the point,* she thought. *The point is, you said you saw them. When Green says they're dead.*

"It didn't do much good to check the logbook for Langley, anyway," added Edwards with too much purpose to his smile. "Sarah's parents' name isn't Langley. It's Serbitt. She was adopted when her own natural parents died. Which she never could get over, according to the Serbitts. Always struggled with it. Nice old couple. Extremely distressed. And while I admire your investigative fervor, Julian, I wish you'd put your energies toward something more useful." He turned, annoyed, and went back into his office. "Check the name. That's the kind of boring police work you've got to learn to do. Don't make assumptions. Check the name."

Adopted when her own natural parents died.

She turned the fact over glumly in her mind.

But why wasn't he more angry?

Because he knew she wouldn't find anything?

Or because he knew it would look worse to try and stop her?

TWENTY-FIVE

Days, she listened. Searching for nuance, for a slip, a hint, for some confirming clue or feeling, in the behavior of Winston Edwards, in the demeanor of Eugene Green. She listened with all of her, her body, her senses, open, tingling, alive.

She would watch Edwards' huge bear-paw hands, search the opacity of those dark eyes, listen to his voice, waiting for something, anything, to convince her one way or the other. To deliver her from this suspended state—open-ended, ambiguous, unanswered.

It brought back, of course—powerfully, freshly—what she'd experienced as a child in the wake of that inexplicable night. Ambiguity. The unanswered. A floating. It had finally receded, that miserable, stinging state of unknowing, evolving from an incapacitating and crushing condition into

... slowly ... a daily way of being, simply a part of her. Subdued, but ever-present.

And here it was, returned. Or at least a mocking echo of it. The same open-endededness. The same not-knowing.

Nights, she lay awake. Playing over and over the moment.

You weren't there. You couldn't know.

Playing over and over, any moment poised with meaning.

The startling interview ...

The dinner in Raleigh-Durham ...

The hallway ...

But the moments were steadily receding, she noticed. Their intricacy, their indelibility, flowing further and further away from her. Night by night, her grasp of them looser, less sure. ...

She had been saved from going further with Edwards. Saved first by confusion, indecision; then, by Green's accusation.

It had put Edwards into a light he would never escape. Something he undoubtedly knew.

She lay on her bed, staring at the ceiling.

In her awkward, unstated, muddling, and undecided way, she had finally and irreversibly said no to him.

He undoubtedly knew that too.

She wondered now what that no might reveal.

What it might unleash.

If it would chillingly clarify the rage she sensed, rage lurking like a predator in the tall grasses, like an adder coiled in the trees.

If her "no" would ultimately prove more revealing of him than her yes ever would.

Days, she looked, listened.

Nights, she couldn't sleep at all.

In Estelle Edwards' immaculate kitchen, before turning in, sleepless, hungry, anxious, Julian surveyed the countertops, sighted a ripe grapefruit, and went to get a knife to halve and peel it. What she saw made her blink, look again, doubting not her eyes but her mind, playing tricks on her in her nervous exhaustion.

She almost laughed aloud, felt like laughing merely for release from the perception.

There was a knife missing from the butcher-block knife rack.

It looked to be the slot for about an eight-inch knife.

"Wounds inflicted with an eight-inch knife." Edwards' booming voice, briefing her that second day.

You're being silly, she thought. *Three in the*

morning, your imagination is running rampant. Relax, for Christ's sake. Relax.

Because while the missing knife made her heart jump, it also made no sense. For if she was indeed dealing with a perfect crime, Winston Edwards style, where would she find the perfect murder weapon?

Not tossed in the park, where someone might quickly find it. Not tossed in the lake or the woods, where it might turn up sooner or later.

But back where it came from, undisturbed, as if nothing had happened. Back in its proper, unsuspected sheath in a country kitchen. Unless it was visibly and irreparably damaged, that sheath in a country kitchen would be the perfect hiding place.

Her training had taught her that, contrary to intuition, a high-quality knife, even a high-quality kitchen knife, could easily inflict all those wounds, and remain—after a thorough washing—pristine and undamaged and in good working order. It was a knowledge that, like her, wouldn't sleep either.

Just then the hallway door rattled. And opened. Julian's heart jumped higher.

Winston Edwards entered. "*Thought* I heard something."

He saw the grapefruit in her hand, and smiled. He looked at the butcher-block slot, frowned, then walked across the kitchen and opened the dishwasher.

He took an eight-inch serrated knife out of the dishwasher. "Ah, there it is," he said. "Some people wash their knives by hand, you know. Worry the dishwasher'll ruin the handle. But I say it gets a knife nice and clean. Don't you think?"

They looked long at each other.

"Split it?" asked Edwards, gesturing with the knife toward the grapefruit.

Bastard. Who are you? What are you doing? Toying with me? Testing me? Trying to rattle me?

"Sure," smiled Julian.

In a moment the only sound in the kitchen was the seemingly contented chewing of grapefruit sections. That, and the insistent thumping of Julian's blood pulsing in her ears.

TWENTY-SIX

"Today, we talk to the press," said Edwards cheerfully, purposefully, in the morning. "Call Art at the *Albany Mail*," he directed her. "Tell him we're ready to see him. Got something for him. Three P.M."

This from the man who had lectured in rage to Eugene Green just days before, on the evil and untruth a free but frenzied press could perpetrate.

Julian sensed she was about to have another lesson: She was about to see, firsthand, how a man gets tried in the newspapers.

"We have a suspect," said Edwards, when she had got Art on the phone, and had switched him, at Edwards' instruction, to the squawkbox.

"And who is it?" said the scratchy speaker-phone voice.

"His name is Eugene Green."

"And how did you finally turn him up?" asked Art with a wariness that seemed to imply some cynical knowledge about Edwards' previous methods.

"He turned himself up. Posing as Wayne Hill, the psychic."

"No. Wait." You could hear the shift in tone: weary to alert. The newspaperman's instinct and hunger kicking in. You could almost see the newsroom chair swivel to an attentive new angle. "You mean that wasn't Wayne Hill I was talking to?"

"That's right."

"Holy shit," said Art.

Edwards told almost all of it. The black pumps that might have appeared white in the moonlight. The torn blue scarf that the psychic had uncannily—too uncannily—summoned up. The fruitless visit to Sarah's apartment. The park visit to the water's edge, where Green had pretended to faint.

He said nothing about the confrontation in Edwards' office, about Green accusing Edwards. And of course he said nothing about the jade necklace, hidden now in Julian's room.

"I've waited a long time for a story like this," confessed Art.

He slurped up all the details like a starving dog.

The article appeared in the evening edition.

Julian blanched to think what the station house would be like by morning.

TWENTY-SEVEN

At night, when the Edwardses' kitchen lights were on, Julian could see the entire kitchen fairly clearly through the woods from her barn apartment. In the constant, ominous wind of the November night, the strong kitchen lighting illuminated the clump of deciduous trees outside it in a strange shivering dance. She imagined she might one night detect Rumpelstiltskin romping around in front of the kitchen's huge gas stove, as if around a raging deepwoods fire.

She awoke at four A.M. to discover that she had finally slept. She watched the shivering dance. The kitchen lights were ablaze.

She heard a faint, high-pitched sound, then silence, then the faint, high-pitched sound again. She would have written it off as some unidentifiable woods animal, but the sound seemed so clearly, so strangely, to come from the kitchen.

Julian got up, pulled her boots on over her bare feet, wrapped the heavy parka around her nightgown, went out, down the steps, and started up the path toward the illuminated kitchen, Gretel in the night.

She drew closer. Then froze.

What she saw through the kitchen window explained, in an incandescent flash, why the puzzle of Winston Edwards and Eugene Green had so confounded her.

Why each had seemed, at different moments, to have both done it and then—protean, slippery—not to have done it.

Why each seemed sometimes to have an excuse, and then to have none.

She now understood why tying the crime to one or the other of them had proved so elusive.

Because neither one of them had done it.

Because through the kitchen window, at four A.M., faced away from her, she saw Estelle Edwards pounding the blade of a kitchen knife repeatedly and furiously into the butcher block.

The same kitchen knife, Julian simply knew, that Julian had noticed missing from the knife rack.

The same knife that Edwards had then removed from the dishwasher.

Estelle Edwards. As massive, as powerful as her husband. Easily enough mistaken for him in the dead of night across some inexplicit distance of a moonlit park.

From every corner of possibility, the logic closed in on Julian in perfect order.

Estelle Edwards had killed Sarah Langley.

And Winston Edwards, her husband, knew it.

In an incendiary moment, it explained everything.

Julian drew closer.

Although she had a compelling and overriding feeling about that knife, she had to see it. Maybe it was a stupid police insistence, a stupid and dangerous literalness on her part. But she had to see it. And Estelle's massive body was in the way.

Estelle's driving of the knife into the butcher block continued unabated.

Julian carefully ascended the creaky back steps.

Old wood. Rusty nails. Step lightly. Lightly. Heel to toe.

Her heart pounded. She felt none of the night cold. Her body was alive with energy, with alertness. Warmth coursed through her. It could have been summer.

Vaguely, instinctively, well-trained, she processed the danger. A woman who had, as it seemed, carefully hidden her crime would be unlikely to attack a tenant in her own kitchen.

On the other hand, the woman was mad, in an insane rage even now, and Julian felt the fear surge through her in an adrenaline rush.

But she had to get a look at that knife.

She leaned forward, to see better from a lower angle, through the lowest panes of the back door's mullioned window.

The step under her moaned, fully, high to low.

Christ.

She saw the knife's pounding suddenly stop. The massive body stood quietly, still faced away from Julian, looking at the knife, not moving.

Estelle had heard her.

Oh God.

With a sudden, deft shift of spirit, a quickly donned cloak of normality, Julian opened the back door. "Mrs. Edwards? Hi. Everything okay?"

Estelle now turned toward Julian, the knife limp at her side. Tears were streaming down her cheeks.

They both stood in silence a moment.

"What's wrong?" said Julian, carefully innocent—and genuinely shocked.

"Everything," said Estelle Edwards, uncalcu-

lating, unthinking. "Absolutely everything," and
the tears poured forth silently anew, a gush of pain
from an endless supply within the stout, enormous
woman. And then, Julian watched—fascinated,
transfixed—as before her eyes, in a heartbeat sor-
row gathered into rage.

"I should kill him," Estelle Edwards screamed,
eyes wide, veins bulging, an electrocution, a mega-
jolt, of fury.

"But . . . how can I?" And she grabbed the
edges of the huge iron stove, as her thick knees
crumpled in exhaustion and grief.

They sat at the kitchen table. Estelle drank water
in gulps, then looked at the glass curiously, as if
into a crystal ball, watching the fluid inside the
glass bend and refract in the harsh kitchen light as
if to read the future, or the truth.

Julian sat mute, a vessel.

Clearly, interestingly, Winston Edwards was
not here now. Where was he? Perhaps Estelle
knew. Perhaps she didn't. Julian wondered, but—
not wanting to jeopardize the aura of late-night revelation—she held the question.

"He was sleeping with that girl," Estelle Edwards said, bitter and unadorned. "He thinks no
one knows, and maybe no one does, but I do."

She spun the glass of water idly in a circle. "He thinks I don't know when he gets up and goes out. Thinks I'm asleep." Estelle looked at Julian, and then simply repeated it. "And he was sleeping with that girl. The Great Chief Edwards."

"You have proof?" Julian uttered tentatively, quietly, and then cringed inwardly. *Too much detective. Not enough friend.*

Estelle smiled bitterly. "I just know, that's all."

Julian drew in her breath, paused, and asked, "And do you think . . . ?"

"Don't even say it, *please!*" said Estelle Edwards angrily. "I can't bear to think that . . ." And then she paused, and said with a pointed, summoned-up, meaningful, and new directness, "It's not him." Estelle looked blankly at Julian after saying it. Then, suddenly, she swigged the rest of the water like a man, shook her head as if to empty all thought and feeling out of it, and, in as labored a way as her husband, arose from the kitchen chair, went out into the hallway, and climbed the narrow staircase back up to bed.

Fear, habit, secrecy, silence, had suddenly reared up out of her rational self, it seemed, to keep Estelle Edwards from saying anything more.

Julian sat alone in the kitchen. The intimate chat of women, the emergence of sisterhood in the wee hours, had only gone so far. She listened for a moment to the house's night noises; its shifting, straining, motherly muttering in the November wind.

Which was it? Edwards covering up his wife's vengeful murder of Sarah Langley? Or Estelle suddenly swigging the water and ascending the stairs, covering up for her husband?

Julian felt all her energy, all her alertness, suddenly drain away. She was nowhere again. Back where she started. Another either/or situation. Another pas de deux. Edwards or his wife. Again, playing two possibilities against each other.

But either way, it was no wonder Edwards had been so alarmed, so enraged, so cornered, by the seemingly "psychic" abilities of "Wayne Hill."

Because he knew just how right "Wayne Hill" was.

And, whether it would ultimately turn out to be Edwards or his wife, Winston Edwards knew who killed Sarah Langley.

And the more Julian considered it, running the facts over the filter of her instinct, the more it seemed that it was not Edwards himself. But instead, the frumpy, immense, bespectacled, powerful-limbed, and raging female double in the bed next to him.

And Winston Edwards would not turn her in. He would defend her to the end, Julian imagined, because he might consider the murder ultimately his own crime. The crime of his affair with Sarah Langley which his wife had come to know of, for which he now must pay.

He might be wracked with guilt over the distress he was causing her. Distress he had caused her repeatedly, if his two A.M. bear-paw reach to Julian in Raleigh-Durham was any indication.

How often *had* he done this?

How often, how deeply, would Estelle retaliate?

She saw, in a plain, raw, unwrapped lesson, what adultery could do. How it could still sear a spouse, even when a marriage seemed, in every sense, to be over anyway. Vaguely, in passing, Julian wondered what would have happened if Estelle had discovered an encounter between Edwards and herself. It was something she chose not to think about too closely. And, thank God, didn't have to.

And at some point, maybe, Estelle Edwards couldn't stand it anymore, and had responded vengefully and ultimately. Not by killing her husband, the revered police chief, but by making him live with the knowledge of the crime. Forever unable to solve it, because he would not hold his wife culpable and accountable—because in his mind, she wasn't, and he was.

They were coconspirators, Winston and his

wife, and neither would say anything about the other.

Edwards was even trying to lead Julian to think it was him, she realized now, to keep her off the scent.

No wonder he was so ambivalent about Julian living here. It wasn't his feelings for her, or what was tentatively between them. That only would have become clearer to both of them, with the increased proximity and time together.

It was his fear of Julian's discovering the truth.

Family first.

Edwards was backcountry, when push came to shove.

It would be touching, thought Julian, if it weren't so sick.

TWENTY-EIGHT

By the next morning, the newspapers were all over the Green/Hill story. Julian rounded the corner of the station house to see news vans parked in the lot, microwave antennas raised high, strange beasts from the future, exploring, alert. There were drivers, photographers, technicians arrayed on the cracked concrete main entrance steps—smoking, joking, rubbing cigarette butts into the creases of weathered concrete whose retaining tar was long gone—exchanging anecdotes, and waiting, waiting, like troops idling in a war zone. In the cold, their breath rose in a silent riot of clouds and mists, hanging momentarily above each of them like sheer dialogue balloons, then disappearing into the thin air.

Inside the station house, bedlam. From the doorway to the second floor, Julian could barely see her own desk outside Edwards' office. Like insects in a grade-B sci-fi film, reporters seemed to swarm over it, as if having gotten a whiff, a taste, they now fairly salivated for more of the story. Julian barely made it across the floor.

"No comment, no comment," she heard herself parrot over and over, feeling like she was in the B movie with them, and hoping, hoping, she would eventually get to say quite a bit more.

Chief Edwards met with them all shortly outside his glass-partitioned office.

"You stand next to me, right here," he instructed Julian, as the press conference was about to begin.

She looked at him doubtfully.

"You solved this as much as me. You were with it right from the start, and every step of the way. You should get the credit."

Honest praise. Another tactic in the mind games of a criminal?

"Gentlemen," he said, then adjusted the greeting appropriately. "Ladies and gentlemen . . ." He paused while they quieted down.

"Yesterday morning at eleven o'clock, Canaanville Police arrested Eugene Green for the murder of Sarah Langley. We have motive—a long-standing relationship, a love affair, between Mr. Green and Miss Langley. We have established beyond the shadow of a doubt, and by his own admission, the suspect at the scene of the crime. We have supporting factors—a history of mental illness, a substantial previous arrest record, numerous fingerprints in the dead girl's apartment that of course match the suspect's. We do not have a murder weapon, which forensics shows to be an eight-inch knife. . . ."

The fluent, forceful, highly organized presentation was in such contrast to his ragged, rugged, normal speech. His chameleon capacities. The ease of deceit. Julian was shocked.

The reporters couldn't sit quiet a second more.

"Is it true that Mr. Green cut off his own last finger to pose as the psychic Wayne Hill?"

"Yes it is. And I will let the unbalance of that act speak further as to Mr. Green's distraught state of mind. To say nothing of his demonstrated willingness to wield a knife—even on himself," Edwards added, with a twinkle of dark humor the reporters seemed to appreciate.

"Cutting off a body part for love. Sort of the van Gogh effect?" mused a gray-haired reporter.

"Call it that if you wish."

The van Gogh effect. They'll have a field day with that, thought Julian.

"How could you *not* know this wasn't Wayne Hill?" asked one young reporter, incredulous, and Julian could see Edwards bristle just slightly, but answer smoothly.

"We had never seen a photograph. His behavior was consistent. He had Mr. Hill's distinctive missing finger. And he gradually displayed relevant and considerable knowledge of the crime. Believe me, the impersonation is a source of great embarrassment to this department."

"Isn't it possible to know whether a scar is new or not? Wouldn't you have seen it was a fairly new scar where Green was missing the finger, and known that something wasn't right?" another reporter asked.

"It is of course well-known that a new scar will have a perimeter of whiter skin around it, and a small skin fold that disappears only with years," said Edwards authoritatively. "Yes, I could see it was a new scar, and that is part of what helped us solve this."

What?! A new scar! And you knew?

"Was Mr. Green posing as Wayne Hill in order to assist in the investigation?"

"Yes, it appears that he was. Whether it was to direct the investigation toward his own purposes, I can only speculate. I will let you make of that what you will," said Edwards.

"And what about the fact that he accused *you* of the murder, Chief?"

Chief Edwards paused.

He hadn't given that little tidbit to Art.

Obviously someone had leaked it.

But Edwards kept his composure, rolled his eyes, and, smiling impishly, said, "I'll also let *that* accusation speak for itself." There were a few chuckles; the reporters smiled knowingly back.

"Conference is over," said Edwards a minute later, and he turned and headed into his office.

And Julian knew she was about to see Eugene Green steamrolled into a cell for a lifetime, and she knew she couldn't just sit and watch it.

"You *knew* it was a new scar, and you didn't say anything!" Julian burst into Edwards' office, steaming, when the reporters were finally gone. "You *knew* it wasn't Wayne Hill, yet you didn't tell me. You left off my education. Why?"

Edwards studied her.

It seemed to Julian that Edwards had slipped. He had goofed. Proud of his skill and experience, in the heat of the moment, he had revealed during the conference that it was an old trick, child's play, to distinguish an old scar from a new one—and his pride in his craft had made him blunder.

"I wondered what he was up to," said Edwards now. "I wondered how he knew what he did. But I was fairly certain, fairly early on, that he wasn't actually psychic. I mean, come on. Which meant he was the killer."

"Or a witness. Just like he said."

She looked at Edwards evenly. Edwards looked just as evenly back at her.

"In which case it would be best," Julian continued, never taking her eyes off Edwards, "to keep him around, wouldn't it, keep him on payroll, figure out what to do with him, maybe even how to engineer him into guilt?" She could barely believe she had said it. The words sounded to her like someone else's. Someone angrier, stronger, more confident.

Edwards looked at her, expressionless. "You're doing it again, Julian. You're going overactive on me. I'm sure you're going to find that in police work, things turn out to be much simpler than they first appear. Out of complexity, simplicity." He raised a thick finger in the air, a gentle, professorial emphasis of the thought.

"Yes, I think you're right about that," Julian said. "I think you're exactly right. Things *do* turn out to be simpler than they first appear." She couldn't contain it any longer. "You don't have enough on Green, and you know it. It wasn't him, and you know that, too. And if this wasn't your corrupt little town, you couldn't hold him. You're absolutely right. Out of complexity, simplicity." She smiled bitterly. "Thanks for resuming my education."

She turned and strode out.

And despite her anger, and even if she hadn't learned any more definitively about Edwards and Estelle and the night of the murder, she had learned something equally and vitally significant, and worth bearing in mind.

That Winston Edwards was perfectly willing to keep things from her.

TWENTY-NINE

While Edwards was further occupied with reporters, Julian found refuge in the one place they weren't allowed to go.

She descended into lockup for a second interview.

This time she brought a handful of current magazines, and, respectful of Green's previously stated reading habits, no newspapers. Was it Eugene Green posing as Wayne Hill who never read the newspapers? Or was it Green himself? Either way, she would demonstrate her respect and attentiveness by bringing other kinds of reading material. Maybe some sympathy would win some trust.

"Tell me about the relationship. *Really* tell me."

Eugene Green looked annoyed at her.

"It's your only chance," Julian said warningly.

Eugene Green stood, went to the tiny window, no more than a slat of light onto the world, a brief note of consideration from some nameless institutional architect or contractor, or perhaps just a nameless, sympathetic mason.

"I loved her, and she loved me," he said simply, into the slat of light. The words, like the thought, had an especial clarity, and his voice—startlingly clear and unraspy at the revelation in Edwards' office—was now, for this moment, even more clear and true. He turned toward Julian. "I don't know that there's anything more important to say than that."

"You're going to *have to* say more. You're going to have to keep talking until I believe you," said Julian.

Green shrugged assent. And began, as if perfectly obediently, to relate it simply, matter-of-factly; and in a few moments Julian found herself unaware of the uncomfortably hard chair she was sitting on, of the bleak light around her, of the dankness of the air she breathed, of the day and time marching relentlessly on around her, while she surrendered and drifted on the words and waves of a man's passion, while she touched and felt along the fabric of a man's soul.

Hard to describe her, he said, because Sarah was the kind of person who, to begin with, you think couldn't really exist. Only in the imagination, and then just barely. But then she happens along in reality and is wilder, bigger, way bigger, than anything imagined. Outsized. Uncontained by the world. Immense appetites and lusts. But starved, too. This small-town beauty, starved and stuck. And because of that, even more eager for life.

How she entered the room, and the room hummed. Hell, the building hummed. You know to stay away, but you can't. Yeah, her looks, sure. Staggering. But this energy. This defiance of limits.

A wildness that made so-called wild girls despise her. A broken puppet, too. Dirt-poor. Abused. Goddamn cretins in her past. But it gave her a soul. It made her real. Which made her even more desirable. If that was possible.

"She . . . I don't know . . . She glowed," he said in the end. "Just glowed. Bright light amid life's muck. . . ."

It was a passion, a devotion, Julian could only hope to know one day, and fully expected never to.

And a richer portrait than Edwards had conveyed. Or was Sarah destined to be drawn differently on every canvas?

Even if it turned out—by some unimaginably strange fate—that Eugene Green *did* kill Sarah Langley, one thing was certain.

Eugene Green loved Sarah Langley.

THIRTY

Julian sat for dinner again with Chief Edwards and his wife Estelle.

They were preserving the ritual.

It was positively gothic.

The discussion ran the gamut of the mundane, built ingeniously on the subjects of the weather, the seasons, real estate, and then, in the full face of the absurdity of the unspoken triangular alliance, sputtered and collapsed into silence.

When Estelle went to the kitchen, Winston Edwards leaned across the table and said, "How are your interviews with Eugene going?"

Julian stiffened, but didn't answer.

"Revealed anything worth knowing yet?" Winston inquired.

Julian dug into her meal more heartily.

"I've been patient with you until now," whispered Edwards. Dishes clattered in the kitchen. "I thought you were my friend. I assure you, I'm much better to have as a friend than an enemy."

A shiver went through her.

But she looked up defiantly at him. "Are you threatening me?"

"That all depends. Are you threatening me?" he asked her, in barely a whisper.

"Did you do it, Winston?" Julian asked him.

"Did I do it, Julian?" Winston asked her, and smiled.

THIRTY-ONE

The arraignment of Eugene Green proceeded in a blur. It was a reiteration, a formalized version, of Edwards' presentation to the reporters. It was not only Edwards' version of events, but often Edwards' very words, Julian noticed, mouthed by the young, carrot-topped prosecutor and no one else, for no one else was necessary. Edwards was the puppeteer, pulling the strings in the courtroom dance with a practiced, almost weary mastery, it seemed; lifting, after a few short minutes, the final string—the judge's gavel—letting it drop to the scarred wooden surface, to accentuate the announcement of the date of trial.

The arraignment of Eugene Green was truly exceptional in its unexceptionality, in its textbook, unchallenged, merciless, machinelike procedure, marked as only slightly unusual by the refusal of Green himself to attend.

She could tell by the efficiency, the predictability of the dance, that the verdict was already in.

"Don't you care?" she asked Eugene Green, who had sunk into an uncommunicative despair. The magazines, Julian saw, remained untouched and unopened in the same pile she had handed him. "Don't you care who defends you?"

He looked up slowly from some sunken place. "You don't quite believe me, knowing all that you do. How could I expect a defense attorney to? Or a jury?" he added morosely.

For his defense, he had been assigned as counsel a lackey of the state. Julian had gone to see the man with her doubts and concerns, but within minutes of meeting him in his tiny office across from the court and advising him of some of her suspicions she could see the look of incredulity, the man's wearisome look that said, *Good lord, am I now going to have to deal with this?*

It was no use. They were readying, methodically loading, to shoot a duck in a barrel. A stooped, beaten, lovesick, already-plucked duck, at that.

She had forgotten for a long moment where she really was. What kind of people she really was dealing with.

Now it came forcefully back to her—the leers of Simms and the others, the vacant idiocy of the Rhine Brothers counterman, the gripping, callous cold of November in forsaken upper New York—and she saw it coldly and crisply, and all too well.

THIRTY-TWO

Arriving at the station house the following morning, Julian detected an indefinable but unmistakable buzz in the air. Her instincts, her fallible but developing instincts, told her something was up.

In the new pattern that had emerged, now there were rarely any words at all exchanged between her and Edwards. She would go silently and sullenly to her desk, Edwards would do the same, disappearing into his glassed-in office, and for his constant visibility would be all the more tauntingly inaccessible.

But this morning Julian had barely reached her desk and set down her purse and coffee before she saw the crooked finger of Winston Edwards summoning her into his demesne.

She entered slowly, and realized upon entering how palpably different the office felt now.

They looked evenly at each other. She could not say anymore what was in his look, in his mind, just as she could no longer say exactly what was in her own.

Edwards then, quite suddenly, leaned far back in the huge, ancient creaking leather chair, and smiled, ever so slightly.

Old times?

"Well, Miz Palmer, I certainly couldn't leave you out in the cold on a development like this one, could I?" he said.

"Development like what?"

"Ah, so you don't know."

"I don't think so," she said suspiciously.

He looked at her, and smiled. "Found a little something. And it ain't shoes. And it ain't blue fabric." He leaned back to the impossible angle in the familiar chair, looked out the dirty plate-glass window for a beat before swiveling his immense head to look at her again. "Found the knife."

What?!

"Eight inches. Serrated."

My God. She knew immediately, felt it all through her. *You planted it out there.*

"Simms found it this morning. Mile down-river."

"What on earth was he doing out there?"

"I sent him."

Julian looked at Edwards, uncomprehending, in disbelief. *How do you think you'll get away with this?*

"You ready for this?" said Edwards, wide-eyed, uncharacteristically excited. "It came to me in a dream."

"What?!"

A dream! Who do you expect to believe that? And it occurred to her, with a sinking feeling, that they all would. *"That's how he's always done it,"* Simms had said. *"Broods and sulks . . . and then one day, lo and behold, he's got the solution."*

Her breath felt short. *You control them. You control them all.* A tightening in her lungs.

But why now? she wondered. Was he afraid she was getting closer? So he needed to quickly tie it up tight?

No. It suddenly hit her. *Now—because now you have a way to make the knife Green's. With a four-fingered print. Now that you have a suspect, you can tailor-fit him a murder weapon.*

He examined her closely, a mix of bemusement and mild frustration. "You don't believe in dreams? In a person's ability to have unconscious insight?"

She regarded him silently.

"Well, I can't blame you, I guess. I wouldn't have believed it, either. Christ, is this ever a strange case." He looked at her, imploringly, innocently. "Look, Julian. I don't know why I dreamed it. I can't explain it. I woke up and thought it was ridiculous. Believe me. But it was so vivid. Like those white shoes I dreamed about. So I figured it couldn't hurt to send Simms out to take a look. God knows, I never thought he'd find anything."

"But you had looked there before," said Julian.

"Right."

"But never found anything."

"That's right. But we were looking for something that had dropped. Just out there, exposed. But the killer hid it. And that's what was in the dream. That the killer stopped to hide it."

"So you sent Simms." *To authenticate it. Make it look good.*

I'm upstate. I'm way upstate.

She was silent.

"Well, believe what you want," he shrugged, insulted. "Or stop believing, if you want."

During Estelle's frantic rage that night, Winston Edwards had been away. And now Julian knew where.

The familiar revulsion, the sickening tide, rose up in her again.

Edwards, she realized, might know that Julian had been in the house that night, and that she was aware of his conspicuous absence, depending on whether Estelle had told him anything about their little wee-hour visit. Probably hadn't mentioned a word. But who could read the twists and kinks and hidden coils of the Edwardses' relationship? Who could know with any certainty?

You're going to taunt us all with this, aren't you? Is this how you're going to go out, Winston? With a joke?

"Where's the knife now?" asked Julian.

"Down in forensics. Got Sam in first thing to work it up." He checked his watch. "Should be ready for us. Care to join me?"

To try to convince me it isn't you or your wife?

Or to show me how you've made your Perfect Crime even more perfect, and even more criminal?

"After you," she said coolly.

Someway, somehow, you are not going to get away with this.

Winston Edwards and Julian Palmer strode briskly down the chipped stone steps toward the ancient forensics lab—used as rarely as the holding cells—in the basement of the building. Next door, in fact, to the holding cells and their lone occupant, Eugene Green.

They burst through the peeling, swinging double doors into the fluorescent-flooded, putrid-smelling room where Sam, the short, unshaven yet cherubic forensics expert, having heard their footsteps and thus anticipated their arrival, held the weapon up triumphantly and on cue.

Julian's heart sank.

"A kitchen knife," he said. "Serrated. Eight inches in length. Same kind of knife, judging by the wounds, used in the Langley murder."

Same kind of kitchen knife she had seen in the Edwardses' dishwasher.

The thought of checking that night to see if the knife was gone from the Edwardses' kitchen had, of course, occurred to her—but immediately, simultaneously, she realized how absurd that was. Edwards certainly would have replaced it.

A swell, a taste of nausea.

She turned to Edwards.

You brought it there, thought Julian, the words shouting in her brain. *You brought it there, and had your obedient human hounds finally stumble on it.*

"And the knife?" said the Chief, focused almost monomaniacally on Sam, she noticed.

"No prints," Sam said.

"None?" said the Chief. He looked crestfallen, confused.

"No," said the forensics expert. "A gloved

hand. Perfectly reasonable, unfortunately, considering this weather."

Chief Edwards looked at the floor, then strangely, almost angrily, at Sam.

"A gloved hand, which means nothing," said the forensics expert. "Normally, that is." And then Sam grinned.

The Chief brightened. "Meaning?"

"Meaning the marks of this glove indicate something rather unusual."

With a theatrical flourish, he switched on the ancient fluorescent light panel on the wall. Edwards and Julian blinked and squinted, finally focusing on a single large negative, about the size of a magazine page, suspended there. Sam gestured them closer, and pointed. "Note only the merest trace—an absence, really—of any fifth finger." He leaned toward the negative, examining it again himself, as if to be utterly, thoroughly responsible, his eyes screwed tightly into a squint, his jaw absurdly slack with his intensity of concentration.

He paused, but Julian already knew.

"The imprint of just four fingers, rather than five," said Sam, looking down, closing his jaw, as if with gustatory satisfaction.

Sam and Edwards smiled at each other.

The sense of drama. The suspended moment. The perfect outcome.

Julian turned away in disgust.

And suddenly back to them. "Wait a second. Just a second. Which hand?"

"Well, hard to say. . . ." said Sam, shifting uncomfortably. "Prints're pretty smudged. . . ."

"You mean you can tell it's four fingers, but you can't tell if it's a right hand or a left hand?"

"Well, I mean, you can't see—"

"Just check the relative length of the index and middle fingers."

Sam bristled. "I know that's how you *would* do it, Miss Palmer. But look for yourself. It's just too unclear. . . ."

She didn't need to. She already had looked. She knew you couldn't tell. She knew he was right. At the Academy, it was sarcastically referred to as "Animal Protection"—meaning severe-enough violence actually hid certain data and clues. Meaning enough beastliness, enough ghastliness, might actually protect you.

Her eyes bored into Edwards'. She felt herself begin to rise to the challenge. "It was obvious from those pictures of Sarah on your wall that first day, obvious to both of us, that despite the unholy forensic mess of that corpse, the preponderance of entry-wound angles clearly indicates a right-hander." She looked at him. He registered nothing. She continued. "I know the preponderance of entry wounds isn't enough to hold up in court. But *you* know it's a right-hander. And *I* know it. And we can't pretend we don't."

There was a brief silence. And then, exceedingly slowly and carefully, Edwards began to speak. "You may know it, Miss Palmer," he said facetiously. "Your Academy training may tell you you know it. But I'm afraid I don't know any such thing." He looked back at her as hard, she noticed, as she had looked at him. "Body in a state like that—forty-four wounds? forty-six? Hell, we couldn't even count 'em. No, can't be too sure about entrance wounds."

"But you can't just abandon the fact—"

"See, what *I* know is much simpler. What I know is that a four-fingered gloveprint was found on this weapon, and a four-fingered fake psychic is down in our holding pen. Call me a simpleton . . . ." He paused. ". . . but I find that juries like it simple, too."

She looked at him. She felt winded. "And you know as well as I do," she said, "that the smudges on that gloveprint are never going to show whether the glove was right-handed or left-handed."

"Too bad, isn't it?" he responded, almost wistfully.

"Works out quite well for you, doesn't it?"

Edwards was silent.

She looked at him.

"You're determined to get Green for this."

"I'm determined to make a murderer pay," said Edwards grandly, formally. "Call me crazy." He slurped his coffee.

The Even More Perfect Crime was looming, and the Bear, it seemed, could taste the honey-sweetness of it.

"Doesn't it bother you?" said Julian, unable to stomach this charade any longer. "Doesn't it bother you in the least, that there was no weapon found, after combing the area repeatedly, and suddenly, there it is?"

"But . . . the dream," protested Edwards.

"Oh, come on, Winston. The area was searched for weeks, and then, suddenly, Simms scoops it up in a minute?" She shook her head in disbelief.

Edwards turned away, insulted, annoyed.

"Doesn't it bother you in the least," she continued, undeterred, "that there are four fingers on the knife, when the man sitting in the jail cell downstairs has four fingers, *and still maintains his innocence?* Isn't the incredible obviousness of that four-fingered gloveprint at all disturbing? Do you think he'd be so stupid as to *want* to get caught?" she asked. "Particularly since he *still* maintains it was someone else?" *You, in fact. You. You.* She felt the urge to shout it, to grab him, to take him by the hair and shake the truth from him.

"Miz Palmer," he said loftily, wearily, as if pained to remind her who was the master and who the student, "the unconscious wish to be caught is a fairly common phenomenon. Something I know you know from that Academy of yours. You've got to admit, a compulsion to be caught would be among the less-strange aspects of Mr. Eugene Green." He cocked his head. "And would certainly seem to be among his less-strange attributes to a jury."

"Doesn't it bother you that Wayne Hill, who we were suspicious about to begin with, is four-fingered as well?"

Rolling his eyes in weariness: "You heard what Tibor told us, and what Tibor's nurse confirmed. The real Wayne Hill is *living at the hospital*, for Christ's sake. And the log-in book at a state facility like that is a lot more conclusive than ours. His time is totally accounted-for. Totally. We've checked that, and you know that. Whatever the case may have been on that unsolved murder, vanishing powers or whatever, he seems to have been far away from this one."

And she knew he was right about that, too.

"No," Edwards concluded, rising, "all these little side issues don't bother me in the least, although I am bothered that they bother you," he said, as he moved back toward the swinging door.

At the door he stopped and turned. "But, just for the record, Miz Palmer, instead of pointing out all these glancing and smoky objections, what would you say the evidence *is*? What would you say we could intelligently speculate, if not safely conclude?"

"That this is the murder weapon from Sarah Langley's murder," she said flatly, mechanically.

"Well, you don't seem very pleased with the discovery of the murder weapon," he said with a sardonic smile.

No. Not pleased at all.

THIRTY-THREE

No fifth finger.

Hill's defect, Green's gothic imitation of it, had been duly carried in the papers. It seemed, not surprisingly, to be their favorite aspect of the case.

At lunch, Julian once again descended to talk to Eugene Green.

Their two worlds—Edwards' and Green's—were separated by about forty vertical feet, Julian calculated, but they were like opposite ends of the universe. Edwards, sitting above Canaanville, in a clean white shirt laid out by Estelle each morning, in his bright, glass-walled office; slanting November sun pouring in through the dirt-crusted windows, splintering the sunlight, making the office on cloudless mornings blindingly bright. And Eugene

Green, wearing the same old dirty outfit, sat occupying this mostly subterranean holding cell, crumbling stone and brown cement, pitch-black but for the struggling dim bulb overhead.

It was a little, municipal version of heaven and hell. Upstairs, morning light streamed through the plate-glass window and, by virtue of the floating dust, looked oddly celestial. Down here, all was bleak and tortured and black.

Which was the heaven and which the hell, however, wasn't clear at all, though it was clear that the man forty feet above her was attempting to play God. And getting away with the impersonation.

"I brought you more to read," said Julian cheerfully, handing Green a stack of magazines.

"And what are you looking for in return?" Eugene Green asked humorlessly.

Julian was slightly offended, but pressed on. "You can't imagine what's happened," she said to Green.

"They found a knife," said Green evenly.

Julian looked at him in amazement. *You're not psychic.* "How did you know?"

Green smiled at her. "He was here."

"Edwards?"

"Early this morning."

"What was he doing here?"

"Came to tell me about it. Thought I'd be interested that it had been discovered, he said. He even had the knife with him."

"He did?"

"Very proud of finding it. Said he hoped this case would be a whole lot easier now. Asked me to hold it."

What?! Fingerprints! He wanted to get your prints on it!

"I hope you didn't hold it."

"Yes."

"How could you!" She got up, and paced, and turned on Eugene Green safe behind his bars. "How could you be so stupid?" She looked at him. "You seem so cagey sometimes—and then . . . so naive!"

Green smiled idiotically at her. "What difference could it make?" He paused. "Resignation could be a sign of intelligence, you know. As the cops like to say—I'm cooperating," he smiled.

"You gave Green the knife!" She stood at Edwards' desk, fuming.

"I wanted to see how he held the knife, that's all," said Edwards defensively.

"You wanted his prints on it," said Julian. Her heart was racing. "You knew there'd only be gloveprints on the knife when it was run through forensics. You knew that gloveprints would be inconclusive, and you've got all Green's prints from Sarah Langley's apartment, and you wanted to get his prints on the knife."

"What are you talking about? The knife already had been to forensics. The gloveprints were already taken. Already registered as evidence. A fingerprint would have been totally contradictory." Edwards looked at her. "I went to see Green *after* that," Edwards said irritably. "Jesus, I wouldn't do that with evidence. And if you think about it, Julian, you know that about me." He looked at her over his bifocals, looked down, shook his head in disappointment. "Aren't you interested in learning about how Green held the knife? Or have you given up on trying to get to the truth?"

She felt chastened. "What did you learn?" she asked.

Edwards shrugged. Looked at her, sighed. "Nothing, unfortunately."

"And what had you even hoped to learn?" she asked after a beat, eyes narrowed, focused intensely on him. *What the hell could you learn?*

He didn't answer.

THIRTY-FOUR

Julian sat alone at the Rhine Brothers lunch counter, the coffee in front of her untouched. The afternoon wind whipped zestful, punchy, wide-awake, and made the plate-glass windows hum.

It had been a puzzle, a complex puzzle in multiple dimensions—Julian, Edwards, Estelle, Green—whose pieces had jammed in place and couldn't be moved.

Had he planted the knife? Or *did* the eccentric genius somehow dream it? His intuition was powerful, uncanny, as he'd demonstrated repeatedly, from the day of her interview to the peeling-away of her past. Julian remembered what Estelle had said at dinner about Edwards' mother. The detail had stuck with her. How Edwards' mother had come up to Estelle on their wedding day, looked just above her head, said, "Three children," and walked away. Was it possible there was some indefinable ability? But no matter: in the final analysis, when she looked purely at the evidence, she didn't have enough on Edwards or his wife to truly convince her it was one of them. Or to convince her it wasn't.

She felt a presence a few stools down from her. She turned.

"I came looking for you," Edwards said. "I want to talk to you."

She looked at him.

"That's the thing about a small town, isn't it? Tough to get away. Everybody's everywhere," he said. "That's what makes me sure the murderer is here among us." He looked at Julian and smiled.

"You planted that knife."

Edwards shook his head in amusement, kept smiling. "Let's say I did. Doesn't make me a killer, does it?" He narrowed his eyes. "And it doesn't mean Estelle is, either." He spun on the stool. "Might just mean I want to go out with a perfect record. Might just be a matter of vanity." He shrugged. "Use my power, at the last second, to achieve a little justice."

"Abuse it, you mean."

"Okay, then, abuse it."

Silence.

"So you'd send an innocent man to jail?"

"Innocent?" He looked at her with startlement. "Don't be so sure."

"Send a man to jail, so certain things, certain relationships, don't come to light."

He shook his head, bemused again, sipped his coffee. "No one'll ever accuse you of being short on theory," he said. Then he put his cup down, and became, Julian saw, suddenly and visibly more serious. "But here's the possibility I want you to consider. Consider the idea, just for a moment, that it wasn't Green, or Estelle, or the Great Chief Winston Edwards. Just consider that for a second." He picked up the cup, sipped. "Who would it be?"

"Are you really entertaining the idea that it was someone else entirely, Winston, or are you humoring me?"

Or maybe you can't help yourself. Maybe you didn't do it, after all. And it is your vanity, holding Green for the moment, but you're still looking. You can't help yourself: you're still looking for the truth.

And just as fascinating, just as interesting to her, was the fact that he'd sought her out to see what she thought, a fellow professional. *A further tactic? Why are you including me?*

"I've no idea who it could have been. But, as you once said, I've got the sense the murderer is among us." She looked at him, though for the moment, she did not necessarily mean him.

"It still could have been Green," said Edwards.

"Yes," Julian agreed. "It still could have been Green. Is that what you really came over here to tell me?"

Edwards smiled.

Or maybe you only want to stay one step ahead of me. Toying with me. But I'll go along. . . .

But why was he bringing this up? He had Green in the holding cell downstairs. Why would he even entertain the idea of someone else, if he didn't begin to believe it?

Or did he? Did he begin to see other possibilities? Had he been—in the forensics lab, brooding in his office, at some level—actually listening to her?

As if he could read her thoughts, he smiled at her. "Consider everything," he said. "Consider everything." He sipped his coffee, oddly delicately, then set it down.

"It's a fiefdom, isn't it?" she said. "You're way up here where no one can see you, where no one pokes their nose in, nobody looks too closely, and after thirty years, you've got a little fiefdom, to do whatever the hell you please."

"Wouldn't you say that's a slight exaggeration?" said Edwards quietly.

"Slight. Not much," said Julian.

He sipped his coffee carefully.

"It's easy to be a genius when you can manipulate the data, isn't it?" said Julian. She stared at her own cup of coffee. It seemed entirely alien. Unrecognizable. "It's easy to be a myth, isn't it, when no one's around to see the reality."

"Not my idea to be a myth."

"Your idea to remain one, though. Keep your perfect record. By prosecuting a man you know didn't commit this crime," she said. "Putting aside, for a moment, the question of who did."

"What makes you so sure I don't think Green did it?"

"That's what you're doing here. It's why you crossed the street."

"Maybe I crossed the street to try to convince you it *was* Green," he said.

Finally she picked up her own cup of coffee. Stared deeply into the brown liquid, looking for patterns in its swirls. Each time she found one, it would change, shift—mutable. "I don't know who it was," she said at last, quietly. "But I know it wasn't Green."

"Why not?"

She looked at him. "Because it was too perfect."

"Too perfect," he repeated.

"Yes."

"Too perfect." Her own words echoed in her mind.

Because who might have been busy nights making things too perfect?

Who was dangling new theories before her, tempting her to rethink her suspicions, to believe in his prudence, in his thoroughness, in his essential and honest police skills?

Who was flattering her by crossing the street, seeking her out to solicit her opinions?

It was almost as if Edwards were taunting her, daring her to catch him.

It was her master class, her individual tutorial in crime science. And people's lives, it seemed, hung on her grade.

THIRTY-FIVE

Before filing it along with everything else, with the mountains of paper on the case, Julian took a last look at the copy of the old newspaper article Richards had sent them. LOCAL PSYCHIC HELPS CATCH KILLER. There they were again in the photograph, the four of them glumly proud, stiff, Rotarian— Chief Richards, Sergeant Stuart Mickel, County First Selectman Otto Ferlinger, and psychic Wayne Hill. The real Wayne Hill.

This frail, faded photograph. Its incidental arrival from Chief Richards' office that day, and Julian's casual glance at it, had started the roil of events that had led to the discovery of Eugene Green.

She looked closely at the photograph once more, before putting it back in the envelope.

Holy shit.

Holy shit!

She hadn't seen it before.

No one had.

It wasn't the real Wayne Hill who caught her eye this time.

It was Chief Richards.

And the gun he was wearing proudly in the photograph in a holster on his left hip: a standard-issue police .38.

Left hip?

She looked closely now at Sergeant Mickel. Beneath the raised contour of his dress coat, she could detect the bulge of the holster on *his* left hip.

Holy shit. My God. She knew, she knew. But fascinated, compelled, letting the evidence mount, she looked more closely at First Selectman Ferlinger. A dark dot—a pen, obviously—emerged from a right-hand pocket of his white shirt.

She looked up from the photograph and through the glass partition, to Edwards at his desk. His starched white dress shirt, from which his own pen emerged, had only a *left*-side pocket.

It wasn't likely that Chief Richards and Sergeant Mickel were *both* left-handed. It wasn't likely the First Selectman had special shirts.

The newspaper had printed the photograph backwards.

She read the caption beneath the photograph

again. Sure enough, she now saw the names were
listed in the reverse order of the people pictured.
The writer had written it correctly, it would seem,
but the paper had printed the photo wrong. No one
in Chief Richards' precinct had even noticed the
names out of sequence with the picture—probably
because they all knew everyone in the photos so
well. And no one here in Canaanville had noticed
anything, probably because they *didn't* know the
people in the photo.

She opened the top drawer of the desk, took
out the ancient magnifying glass she had laughed
at earlier, held it up to Richards' and the sergeant's
silver nameplates. The printing on them was too
small to see. But what difference did that make,
when the silver nameplates were pinned on the
right breast, instead of the correct left one, as every
cop knew, even in Richards' upcountry jurisdiction.

As an inexorable, powerful chain of logic and
explanation came to her, she smiled to herself.

She had it. She had what she needed. The puzzle pieces had budged and settled into a new and
satisfying pattern, and she couldn't wait to get to
Edwards with it.

Poor Green.

Cutting off that finger had cost him.

Now it was going to save him.

THIRTY-SIX

She burst into Edwards' office, breathless, holding up the newspaper photograph, realizing only then she had done this before—brandished this same photograph just days ago—initiating the whirl of events that had followed.

"The photograph . . ."

She handed it to him.

"Look. Wayne Hill's finger. Missing from his left hand. Same as Eugene's. Correct?" She paused for drama. "Wrong! The photograph is printed backwards! So, Wayne Hill is actually missing the finger from his *right* hand. Green cut his finger off the wrong hand!"

Edwards looked closely at the black-and-white newspaper photograph. Moved it under his nose carefully, attentively, like a microscope slide. Then looked up, slowly, at Julian. The broad features of his face seemed to gather together somehow. In interest, it seemed. Extreme interest.

"See, we never asked Richards what hand Hill's finger is missing from," she continued. "Why would we? We'd seen the newspaper photograph! And Richards hadn't volunteered the information. Why would he? He'd sent us the photo. Who'd ever question it anyway? Obviously it's the same finger. . . . But it isn't."

Edwards stared dumbly at the newspaper photograph. He looked up at Julian, shook his head, confounded. "How could he—how could anyone—screw that up?"

"I think I know," said Julian quietly.

"I don't read the papers," Green had said.

The stack of magazines Julian had brought him, still unopened.

Room 132? Or 123? Couldn't find his room that first night in the Ramada.

Wouldn't sign his name. Another affectation, they'd assumed.

"Eugene Green is dyslexic," she said. "Severely."

"Dyslexic . . ." repeated Edwards, numbly.

Her eyes bored into Edwards' with aliveness. "Don't you see? Poor, dyslexic Eugene Green—despite all his preparation for the impersonation—when the big moment came," her heart was pound-

ing, "followed the photograph in front of him—
this one, the only known photo, the *only* evidence
this overly cautious severe dyslexic could check
himself against, to be sure he'd get it right. He's
smart enough about his dyslexia to know he can't
trust his own memory of Hill's hands, so he works
from the absolute certainty of a photograph. And
what's the result? What does he do? He cuts his
finger off the wrong hand!"

The Chief, looking up at her, leaned back in
the ancient chair, and was in a moment absolutely
motionless.

She had, Julian knew, Winston Edwards' full
attention.

"So . . ." Julian stepped back from his desk.
"What have we got? A four-fingered gloveprint,
and entry-wound angles of a right-hander." She
turned to the gruesome photographs on the wall of
Edwards' office, placed back up by Simms, at Edwards' direction, since the incarceration of Green.
"You may not want to say it aloud in the presence
of anyone who matters, but if *I* immediately knew
it was a right-hander when you first showed me
these, then certainly *you* know it." She kept her
back to him as she said it, as if by not looking at
him, he could not challenge her on it. "Point is,
there's a four-fingered gloveprint on your *supposed*
murder weapon; these wounds indicate a right-

hander; and the man in the holding cell downstairs is four-fingered on his *left* hand." She turned now, looked at him, and said as simply, as directly as she could, "Eugene Green didn't do it. Eugene Green didn't kill Sarah Langley."

Edwards smiled palely, and said quietly, "I know."

"You what?"

"I knew Green had cut his finger off the wrong hand."

"How could you?! The photograph?"

"I'd've never figured it out from the photograph. I've got to give you credit on that one, Julian. No, I know because Richards happened to mention Hill's right hand on the phone."

"When was this?"

"Well, it was obviously a conversation you didn't hear."

She looked at him, dumbfounded.

"Complex-seeming things usually turn out to be quite simple," he said with a smile.

"A conversation you didn't hear." "You didn't tell me," Julian said, still stuck on it, dazed. "Why?"

Winston Edwards shifted his gaze away, out the window to the cornice of Rhine Brothers, and shrugged. "It was something else I held back. That's all."

"Like the blue scarf."

"Yes. Like the blue scarf."

And the jade necklace, she would have added coolly, but somehow she felt this trump card, this trump card she did not yet understand, was meant to be saved.

"Look, I admit it," said Edwards, explaining. "I wanted Green down there in the box, rattle him just enough to see if anything shook loose. And I needed to keep him there long enough for the newspaper reports to get out, and make the real suspect feel secure, too secure."

She looked at the broad, mottled face. And noted just as clearly what was ugly, mean-spirited, manipulative, behind it. What had she seen there? How had she ever seen anything?

"You know I use unorthodox methods, Miz Palmer. Why do you continue to be surprised?" He leaned back. The ancient chair squeaked in protest. "You know I don't believe in getting bogged down in procedure," he said, smirking.

"It's not that you held it back," said Julian. "It's that you held it back from me."

Why? wondered Julian. *Because I'm getting too close?*

"Everyone around me knows how I work," Edwards said curtly. "Everyone knows I'm after the truth."

"You might not know it," he'd said, *"but under these two hundred sixty–some-odd pounds and shabby suits, I've got my vanities."*

She thought of the possibility again that Winston didn't hold things back because it was his tried-and-true technique. But that he held things back to solve it himself. To be a hero. To garner the glory, preserve the legend. Was it that, faced for the first time with the prospect—the thin but real possibility—of sharing the limelight with some young Academy recruit, he simply couldn't stand the idea? Was it all simply ego? Enormous ego?

Or had she concocted this explanation of his not sharing the clues because it was a much more palatable reason than the real one? The darker reason. The simpler reason. The one she was at some level still having trouble accepting.

Complex-seeming things usually turn out to be quite simple.

"I think you want to stay one step ahead of me," she said. And felt, in saying it, its other, more sinister meaning: *Because you need to stay one step ahead of me.*

He's stalling, she thought. *Dancing. Vamping*

for time, putting together another story, another version.

"You didn't know about the wrong finger," Julian said.

"I just told you. Richards mentioned it on the phone."

"You can't hold him. You can't hold Green legally," said Julian. And this time it wasn't a mere observation. Her challenges to the Great Chief's questionable methods were growing more direct.

"Well, I'm not going to hold him forever, for Christ's sake." He looked at her. And she thought she detected what she had longed to feel from him. A hint, a whiff, of his own fear.

She felt stronger with him. Continually stronger. The revulsion, the nausea, were memory now. And she was faster, younger, thought more quickly, than the Old Bear. It was a powerful feeling, that led her powerfully to her next point.

"Well, Chief Edwards," said Julian, standing, brushing her shoe idly but affirmatively twice on the beat-up linoleum floor. "Tell you the truth, I wish you *hadn't* known about Green's cutting off the wrong finger." She looked at him. "See, if you thought Green had used his left hand, you'd be off the hook."

She turned her eyes away, looked out at the roof of Rhine Brothers in Edwards' own accustomed style. "The killer—the *real* killer, if it wasn't the real Wayne Hill—is almost certainly someone trying to imitate him. A four-fingered gloveprint. Pretty damn distinctive, after all. But see, I think the real killer *knew* that Hill was missing the finger from the right hand"—she looked meaningfully at Edwards, skewering him with her eyes—"and *that's* why we find four-fingered prints and wounds of a right hand." Julian stared at him. He looked back—expressionless, vacant. "And," she concluded, "*you* know the murder was by a right hand, as well as I do."

She turned crisply, to exit Edwards' office.

"Wait a second," said Edwards.

She turned back.

"Wait a second," he said again. "That's it, Julian," the excitement growing in him. "Christ Almighty. You've got it!" He looked at her, it seemed, in some mix of astonishment and admiration.

"What?" She was stunned.

"It's just what you said—imitation . . . imitating Hill . . . Yes!" He looked beyond her, to some magical and revelatory point beyond her. "Think, now. That phone call, when I was on the phone with Tibor in the next office, trying to figure out who the hell Green really was. Tibor told me that Green was in the habit of stealing reports, reading other patients' files. Remember?" Edwards asked aloud, excited.

Julian nodded slowly. "Yeah . . ."

"Well, if someone's stealing reports, wouldn't you comment on the fact that they couldn't read?"

"Jesus, that's right," she said. "Why didn't he mention that Green couldn't read?"

"Maybe Tibor didn't know." Edwards' excitement was transformed into a meditative concentration, and he continued with the thought, letting it run like a stream, finding its way to fertile ground. "Maybe Tibor *didn't* know. Maybe looking at the news-story photos of Green these past couple of days, he suddenly saw Green was missing the finger from his left hand. Maybe he realized only then, seeing Green's mistake and adding it to a lot of other evidence from Green's therapy that never added up, that Green was dyslexic. Shit, people can hide all kinds of things from their shrinks. And look, Green hid it from us, after all—a couple of detectives. Hell, we didn't even know Green was Green. The guy is good," said Edwards.

He studied the Rhine Brothers building's roof. "Maybe Tibor didn't realize about the dyslexia until after seeing the newspaper . . ." And he looked up at Julian. "And maybe by then, it was too late."

"Wait a second. What are you saying?"

"Maybe Dr. Tibor figured his ingenious patient Green would cut off the correct finger, and he figured wrong."

And she saw now what he was implying, and it was laughable. Desperate. "Oh . . . Now, Winston," Julian said. He seemed suddenly childlike to her. "So he discovered his mistake about the dyslexia. Professional failure. But Jesus, Winston. . . ." She shook her head. He was grasping. She felt sorry for him. "Jesus, it doesn't make him a killer. There's no motive."

There's no motive. This is ridiculous. You can't turn his professional failure, a little incompetence, into a murder.

"You don't see what I'm saying," said Edwards harshly, excitedly, looking directly at Julian. "Maybe he figured really wrong."

THIRTY-SEVEN

"Simms!" Edwards yelled out his office door.

Docile, gap-toothed, eerie, Simms materialized in front of them.

"Call Sandy Merrick at Rochester Airport Police. Ask him to tap in for a manifest on Dr. and Mrs. Ernest Tibor, travel to the Bahamas, early October. Write down the dates, bring 'em here."

"Yessir," Simms said, turning obediently, hopping to.

He reentered the office a minute later, handed a slip of paper to Edwards.

Edwards squinted at it. "Mrs. Arlene Tibor. Depart Rochester Airport October seventh. Ten-fifteen A.M. Arrive Nassau, Bahamas, October seventh, four-thirty P.M. Dr. Ernest Tibor. Depart. Rochester Airport October eighth . . ." He stopped suddenly, stared at the paper, then looked up at Julian. "A day later. My God."

Huh.

"Maybe he had an appointment," offered Julian weakly.

"I'll say."

He crumpled the slip of paper, thumbed furiously through a stack of papers on his desk, found the phone number he was looking for, dialed the phone, put it on the squawkbox as it rang, turned to Julian, and held his index finger to his lips.

"Dr. Tibor's office," said a nurse's voice.

"Hi, it's Chief Edwards, I don't know if you remember . . ."

"Sure I do. Dr. Tibor's vacation in October, right? A month in the Bahamas. I 'member how jealous you sounded. Plus, I seen your picture in the paper."

"Yes, well, we're just finishing up some details and paperwork on the case for the courts, and we need to have everything neat and tidy and in front of us—you know how that is—so I've got to ask you one more time, to look up Dr. Tibor's vacation schedule."

"Sounds like you guys keep records like we do."

"Well, we're—"

"Lucky for you, the doctor's meticulous. Got

his datebook right here. October, October . . . There it is, October seventh, the Bahamas. Big exclamation point. Return November seventh. Lucky dog."

"And October eighth? No appointments?"

"Weren't you listening? Like I said, October seventh, the Bahamas. Guy was outta here."

"Thanks."

Edwards looked at Julian again.

"On October eighth, his wife in the Bahamas thinks he's on his way from the office. And his office thinks he's already in the Bahamas."

But it would make no sense, Chief. You're grasping at straws. You stumbled into a one-day discrepancy, a change in travel plans, it could be for anything. There's no reason it would be Tibor. No reason at all.

"What if . . .," said Julian, "what if—," she smirked, "I can't believe I'm saying this, but I'll just entertain it, humor you for a moment. What if it *is* Tibor? Well, he's gonna hear from Nurse Ratched there that you were asking those questions. He'll know you know."

"I had no choice," said Edwards. "I can't ask her not to say anything. Then she certainly would. My best chance is saying it's routine and hope she forgets. And if she *does* mention it, he's either going to take off for parts unknown, from which we'll retrieve him, or he'll call us and weave some elaborate story."

Like you're doing, Chief.

"Or take some other summary action, which'll confirm our suspicions for us," said Edwards.

Our suspicions? What suspicions? "It's so . . . far-fetched," Julian said finally, exasperated. "There's just no *reason*," she pointed out to Edwards—angry, and yet oddly, feeling sorry for him, too.

She fully expected to hear a contradiction, some arrogant, hopeful last-ditch effort.

Instead he turned to her—tired, old, weary-looking. "No, you're right," Edwards agreed, suddenly quiet, crestfallen, an aura of moroseness. "There's just no reason."

His eyes searched the cluttered desktop, aimless, desperate, grim. Suddenly she could see the old man in him, confused, disoriented, lost. Laboriously he lifted his eyes. "You need to talk to Eugene again," he said.

"Why don't you?" she asked.

"I can't. You know that my seeing him would only enrage him further. I'd get nowhere."

"You're flouting the law, keeping him there."

"Please, Julian. We need to hold him just a little longer."

So that you can find some other way to pin it on him?

"You have his trust, Julian. Talk to him."

"But he's told me everything he has to say."

"But he hasn't told you the truth." He looked at her imploringly. "I'm telling you. He hasn't told you the truth."

Julian was downstairs in minutes.

The magazines were still piled on the stand in Eugene Green's cell.

Too depressed to read? Yeah, right.

She smiled at Eugene Green, feigned cordiality. But she was seething. If he had duped her on this, how much more had he misled her on? While making it seem that he was confiding, so passionate, so anguished . . .

Pretending pleasantry, making small talk, she pointed to the *People* magazine on the top of the pile, squinted at it in the poor, angled jail-cell light, and asked casually, "What does that headline say?"

Green picked up the magazine, held it closer for her to read.

Anyone might have done it. A perfectly reasonable solution. Boy, he was smooth.

"I don't have my glasses," she said in a cool countermove. "What does it say?"

"It's about Pamela Anderson."

The photograph was of Pamela Anderson. The headlines were about John F. Kennedy Jr. and Pope John Paul.

Julian cooled a little, when she saw the effort Green went through to conceal his incapacity. She took a deep, calming breath, looking at him squarely. "Eugene, for a man who was willing to expose himself to enormous risk for the woman he loved, you certainly go to great pains to hide your dyslexia."

Eugene Green looked back at her, mute, shocked. Then he smiled with sly pride. He picked up the newspapers, thumbed through them absently, brow furrowed. He might have been a suburban father on Sunday morning, sorting the sections of the paper.

"Why didn't you tell me?" Julian asked.

He continued to thumb the newspapers. "You have no idea how it feels, Miss Palmer."

"It's just . . . I wish you'd leveled with me. Because it was the lie, the little lie, that was our first problem together. What do you expect me to think, when you pile lie on lie?"

"What difference does it make what you think, Miss Palmer? Obviously not much. Since I'm still here."

In his cell, Green walked over to the slat of

light high in the wall, the stonemason's momentary sympathy or his structural joke. He squinted his eyes, as if to see farther out of it, and spoke so quietly that Julian strained to hear him. "When I was growing up, mothers still switched left-handers to right. Or at least they did in that sorry backwater," he said, barely above a whisper. "Most mothers, I'm sure, tried it gently but firmly. Encouraging but persuasive. Mine, though, did it the way she did everything. With a vengeance." The light knifed across his face.

"Somehow it became the focus of what was wrong in her life, in ours, in everything. If she could make me right-handed, she seemed to think, everything would be fine." He laughed bitterly. "She acted sweet, nice, loving, with all the trouble I caused. All my scrapes. And then, on the switching of the hands, she became a monster. She focused everything there. And it became rather charged, rather pathological, as old Tibor would say.

"Other things I can learn almost instantly. My memory is almost photographic. My abstract reasoning tests off the chart. But I've tried learning to read a dozen times, and I can't. Not even nursery-school recognition of the letters." He looked at her. "She fucked me up, Julian. The woman fucked me up good."

"Eugene."

"Yes."

She gulped. "Can you tell right from left?"

He turned beet-red; said nothing; looked for a moment, there in his cell, like an embarrassed child.

"Can you?"

Eugene Green stared at her defiantly, turned away.

He would not deign to answer. But by not giving the answer, he was answering. And they both knew it.

He can't tell right from left.

And a thought skimmed across her consciousness, lightly, vaguely, half-formed. . . .

If you can't see right or left in your mind's eye, then what exactly can you see?

"I'm telling you. He hasn't told you the truth," Edwards had said.

Aboveground, the November wind had blown gale-force all day, brutal and unrelenting. Down here, buried in the earth, there was but a slight whisper of it, a ghostly echo of wind, wending its way in through the bricks. It was an almost-perfect silence. Silent enough to think in.

Eugene Green looked out the window again. "What kind of a man could do that to someone?" said Green quietly, and paused self-consciously after saying it, as if to insinuate the sentence into her thoughts. He looked at Julian alienly, confused, as if he had no idea who she was, or who he was, or of anything, momentarily. Then something— maybe the horror of those images, of bearing those images—made Eugene Green's thoughts leap into another compartment of his mind, another place entirely. "I loved her," he said simply, with a shrug. He held his gaze on her, benign, unjudging yet examining. "Do you know what it's like? Have you ever loved someone?"

She tried to picture her father. The picture would not come. That never had happened before. It shocked her, grieved her. Maybe it was the dark, the dankness, the distraction . . .

"What is it?" asked Green.

"Nothing." She shook her head.

There. The arms: brown, warm trees of flesh. Hands like a platform. Swinging her free in the fragrant spring air. The beat of his breathing, sweet, steady, regular, a clock of rushing air, a pulse of life.

But she was losing the picture, she realized. *Losing the picture. . . .*

Green went even quieter. A mumble. A groan. "I sit down here, and watch it. Over and over. It's
can do." The dark, the damp, were taking their
ver and over. Every blow." He shook his

head metronomically. "Do you know what that's like?" His voice rising from nothing—sudden, threatening, but a threat only to himself, of ripping apart, crumbling, crumpling his own being. . . .

Julian was surprised to feel the wetness in her eyes, dewy, a mistake, a strange invasion of delicacy and humanity here in the holding cell.

Do I know what that's like? Yes. Yes I do.

She felt alone. Alone. She thought of Estelle. Big Estelle. Gross. Unloved. The female—but not feminine—version of Winston Edwards. Could you feel alone enough, unloved enough, to kill? Of course. Why not? For all Green's testimony that he had seen Edwards that night in the park, Julian's suspicion about Estelle—Estelle having done it— could still hold. From a distance, Green could have thought Estelle was Winston. Particularly if, from such a safe and therefore deceiving distance, Green had followed her to the Edwardses' home. Of course he would have concluded it was Edwards, the Great Chief, and not Edwards' wife. That would have been unthinkable.

Wait a second.

Given everything Green had s
could have been Estelle. Much of
was consistent with that. And if G
seen Estelle through the trees, rath

couldn't he have mistaken the murderer's identity entirely?

"So how *do* you see it?" she asked Green now, spurred by her thoughts; and the question came so fast from her it seemed almost physically to throw him off balance. It was useless to ask it, maybe mean, surely a laughable question given the circumstance, yet she asked anyway. "Right hand or left hand?"

He looked at her, stunned, then flushed red with rage before her. "Both hands!" he yelled, leaning back into the question forcefully, as if to dominate it, disarm it, push it down. "I see it both ways! Don't you get it? *I'm dyslexic!* Right, left, left, right! I see it happen *every way!*"

The echo pulsed in the subterranean chamber. An aural attack. Her ears actually stung.

If you see it both ways, maybe you didn't see it at all.

"Eugene?"

"What?!" he said, not even listening.

She asked it low, direct, with all the directness that had served her in dealing with Eugene Green. Said it low, direct, so there'd be no echo, no mistake. "Did you see it?"

"See it?! I see it *now*, for Christsake, every moment, over and over . . ." A sackcloth wail, a public mourning, a herculean grief.

She held fast. "But did you *see* it?"

"See it?! I didn't have to see it! I know he did it! And so do you!!"

She asked once more, low, monotone, impervious, a needle, a pinprick, annoying, relentless—though it was killing her inside to ask again, to break this man further.

"Did you see it?"

"You saw how he looked at her high-school picture! How he carried it in his wallet!" The words bouncing off the vaults in a hundred directions, a sonar confusion.

"Yes, but I'm ask—"

"You saw he had her pictures splayed on his wall! *I had to get them down from there*! So I told him to take them down, remember?!"

"Yes, but . . ." She couldn't go on. The pictures. For the moment she'd forgotten the pictures. The nausea—the familiar nausea—now rising up.

She seemed to be doing, finally, fully, what Edwards had asked: remembering, feeling, that this was a real person, a real girl . . .

"*He was sleeping with her! Sleeping with Sarah!* I didn't have to see it! I got there too *late* to see it, you stupid cunt! I was too *late!* Do you think I would have let it happen? After all this talk, after all this time, do you really think I'd have let it happen?! NO, I DIDN'T ACTUALLY SEE IT.

WHAT FUCKING DIFFERENCE DOES THAT MAKE? HE WAS HER LOVER! I KNOW HE DID IT!"

She winced in the verbal onslaught.

So, Green knew Edwards was sleeping with Sarah Langley.

So, Green *hadn't* actually seen Edwards do it.

Two more revelations than she'd been expecting.

Julian was shaking.

THIRTY-EIGHT

"What were you able to learn from Green?" Edwards asked.

"Nothing, really," said Julian, as if ashamed and disappointed in her failure.

Holding back.

His little apprentice was learning fast.

"What did you talk about?"

"More of the same, I'm afraid. His certainty that it was you. His love for Sarah. . . ."

But what have I been learning, Winston? I've been learning to read the ingeniousness of your deceit.

The more she had thought about it, the more ridiculous and hollow Edwards' speculations about Dr. Tibor seemed. Not only did Dr. Tibor have no motive, but now, having Edwards' affair with Sarah revealed by Estelle, and now confirmed by

Green, there was someone—someone just across this metal desk—who clearly did have a powerful and passionate connection to the deceased, which translated very directly into motive.

Of course, Green now had a motive for killing Sarah, too—the discovery that she was two-timing him—but somehow it seemed more likely to Julian that he would have tried to kill Edwards first. Or, in a Eugene Green–like rage, the both of them.

"Chief?"

"Yes."

"About Dr. Tibor . . ." she began, pausing after saying the name, half hoping, half expecting, that Edwards would snap to his senses, snap from his folly, emerge from behind his wafts of smoke and hall of mirrors, from the absurdity of even bringing up the doctor's name. "I mean, look how forthcoming he was in your phone call with him. Look how much he *did* tell you about Eugene Green. Enough for you to charge Green with murder, after all." She looked at Edwards dubiously. "A discrepancy in a vacation schedule. A professional failure—or maybe just an oversight—about the dyslexia. Come on, Chief. . . ."

She searched the broad face for some sign, some twitch of guilt, or humanity, or recognition of the absurdity. *It's a straw you're groping at, Chief, and I'm going to make it the last one.*

But Edwards seemed to be paying no attention, seemed to be caught in some annoying distraction; and then, his mild sense of distraction and annoyance suddenly focused—

"Wait a second, wait a second, wait a second. . . . Go back now, back to the very beginning. To how Eugene told you he met Sarah Langley. Remember?"

Julian looked suspiciously at Edwards. "Eugene and Sarah met at Zimmern Upstate," she said.

"Right! And what did Eugene say Sarah was doing there?"

"Getting some help, over the deaths of her natural parents."

"But he never did say what kind of help, or with who," said Edwards. "Well, if Eugene met Sarah at Zimmern Upstate, and Eugene was Dr. Tibor's patient, who do you think Sarah was there seeing?"

The connection did seem obvious. "Dr. Tibor, I guess," she conceded.

She was starting to sense something, a possibility, a hint of blue sky after rain. . . .

"And maybe Eugene, poor, newly lovestruck Eugene, didn't really understand the nature— meaning the *full* nature—of Sarah's visits," Edwards said.

Eyes narrowed to a twin-barreled weapon, she

aimed all her suspicion, all her doubt at him, and yet there was some insistent possibility, some crazy logic beginning to form.

"Tibor, involved with Sarah? By the time Green met her, involved with her already?"

"Exactly."

Impossible. Outlandish. And something in its impossibility, its outlandishness, was calling out to her. It was completely absurd. And something in its absurdity made it completely plausible.

"Meaning she was soon sleeping with Tibor and Green at the same time."

And with you, Winston?

Jesus.

The most unfathomable player in the drama was turning out to be not the textured, layered Edwards or Green, but the even-more-opaque Sarah Langley. Of course, Edwards didn't realize Julian knew the surprising, lustful sum.

She had to admit, if little Sarah was sleeping with Green and Edwards at the same time, why not her psychiatrist too? Going from one to two was the big psychological step. Two to three or more— that was nothing. You were already gone. Already dead. Sarah was a type Julian would come to recognize in police work, and would never truly understand.

Julian's eyes narrowed again. She spoke very

slowly, very deliberately. "Gee, Chief Edwards, this seems to presuppose an awful lot about the character of Sarah Langley." She feigned shock, horror, a high moralism, all at once. "That this innocent young woman would be involved with one man, and get knowingly, simultaneously, *immediately*, involved with another?" She tried to say it without irony, without sarcasm. "What would make you think—what would tip you off—that she'd be that freewheeling with her affections?"

She looked at him, daring him to say something. "Not quite the innocent girl of the high-school photo you originally sketched for me."

He turned away and continued pretending nothing had been said. "Follow me here, Julian. What if, when Eugene met her, she was already seeing Tibor on a more-than-professional basis? What if Green—not knowing about Tibor and Sarah—*did* get involved with Sarah? Let's face it, neither of *them* would have said anything. Tibor can't admit he's involved with a patient. And Sarah—" His features narrowed. "We all know Sarah isn't particularly truthful on matters like this."

Admitting the affair. Admitting it, at last.

He pressed on. "It would be reasonable to expect a man in therapy sessions, happily, giddily, to begin to tell his shrink about his new love, Sarah

Langley. Never imagining he was shocking his psychiatrist in a way he couldn't know. And then, when Sarah, despite Tibor's threats, refused to break it off with Green, Green never imagined that he was steadily, session by session, driving his psychiatrist crazy."

"Jealousy," said Julian. "Awfully ancient motive, after all this complexity," she said.

"I don't have to say it again, do I?" asked Edwards. *Out of complexity, simplicity.* He leaned back, became professorial, reflective. He paused, arched both eyebrows, as if to clear way for a thought. "Sarah, in her own sessions or in bed, may even have innocently mentioned Green's practice impersonations of Wayne Hill to Tibor. And armed with that knowledge, Tibor—a psychiatrist, after all—may have perceived a use, a clever, eventual use, for Green's fixation on Hill. Because a fixation can go too far. Something a psychiatrist certainly knows. And a fixation"—he leaned forward—"is eagerly imagined by law enforcement, by jurors, by the powers that be, to have gone too far. Which is something about law enforcement, and jurors, and the powers that be, that a psychiatrist who regularly sees criminals knows quite well."

He paused, as if to let the full meaning sink in.

"*That's* why I think Tibor knew he could kill her," said Edwards finally. "Kill her in the style of

Hill, or of Green's impersonation of Hill gone too far, and get away with it.

"He would ask her one more time to break it off with Green, ask her one more time to come run away with him, confront her when his office assumed he was already on vacation, and when his wife assumed he was attending to an appointment; and if that confrontation went sour, well, then he would kill her—kill her in just the way that Hill or Green impersonating Hill would do it. And inevitably—as psychiatrist to both of them—he would assist in, help shape and direct, the police investigation of either one of them, or both, and no one would ever know."

Edwards was silent.

"Two people to take the fall," Julian realized. "Hill *and* Green. Clearly we'd think it would be one of them."

Edwards nodded quietly.

It was quite a performance.

Her hostilities toward him, her defenses, melted a little.

But it was all pure theory, of course. Pure conjecture. And even within that conjecture, there was still something ineffable and vague nagging at her. "Okay. I can see how Tibor himself *could* have killed Sarah Langley. It's possible, I guess. The four-fingered gloveprint, to imitate Hill or Green. But, a psychiatrist . . . the violence of it . . . I just don't think—"

Edwards' eyes widened. "Jesus, you're right!"

She looked at him questioningly.

"You're absolutely right! Tibor didn't kill Sarah Langley!"

"But—"

"*Hill* did. The *real* Wayne Hill. Of course. . . . Look: Who provided Hill's alibi? Tibor, right? Sessions. Sign-ins. All Hill's time, totally accounted for. Now, why the hell would he do that, when if he *hadn't* done it, Hill would be a likely suspect, putting Tibor at less risk? Well, I'll tell you why. And I'm willing to bet the whole Hill alibi is faked.

"He's a psychiatrist, right?" said Edwards. "Professor of human nature. Meaning, presumably, he recognizes his own limits. And the lack of such limits in some of his Zimmern patients. And if it came down to him or Hill, he knows who's going to make the better murderer."

"But . . . how? How on earth could he get Hill to—"

"I'll get to that. Point is, once the murder is done, Tibor, expert on these matters, can, when the time is right, assist in the investigations of Hill, of Green, whichever. Help put them away.

"But Tibor never needed to assist, see? Because like an idiot, I charged Green. So Dr. Tibor never even had to turn Hill over for it. All he had to do was stand by an alibi. A lot simpler. And less risky."

"Jesus Christ," said Julian.

Edwards turned, looked once more out the window to the familiar roof of Rhine Brothers across the street. "So the real question becomes, if Wayne Hill did kill Sarah Langley, what kind of role did Tibor play?"

He squinted. "We don't know all the reasons for one's seeing a psychiatrist," said Edwards. "But if you kill someone, and you're even halfway in your right mind, the guilt is going to play on you. What if Hill is seeing a psychiatrist to *begin* with, because of the guilt—I mean, the loss-of-powers thing, that's just the public version of the story, let's say. Let's say he's seeing the shrink for a *real* reason—intolerable, soul-wrenching guilt."

"The unsolved murder upstate," Julian said, slowly realizing. "The one he couldn't solve . . ."

"Exactly. The unsolved murder upstate. Maybe he confessed it to Tibor right away. More likely, it took awhile: We know, after all, that Hill's been seeing Tibor for over a year. But when he finally brings himself to confess, this shrink, in all his professional wisdom and paternity and authority over his patient after all this time, sees an opportunity, has his own little murderous need developing, and from his position of trust and authority, assures the patient that he shouldn't feel guilty. That there's nothing to feel guilty about. Knowing full well this will never work. Because he knows—hell, he has *proof*—that the patient can't contain the guilt. He knows the 'treatment,' or lack of it, will be ineffective; that this tremendous guilt, having tried to express itself and failed, will have to try to express itself again. And knowing the patient as he does at this point, he knows the patient might even, therefore, seeking to be caught, kill again." He paused. "Something, he knows, will have to give."

He turned back to her. "Or at least that's how it will look, that's how the psychiatrist will present it, when there *is* another killing." He stared. "As if the killer couldn't stand the guilt and seeking to be finally caught, recommitted the crime—this time leaving an unmistakable clue, a four-fingered glove—for which he's the only one fitting the description. An unmistakable clue, saying, 'Catch me, find me, end this ordeal.'

"That's how it will look, the psychiatrist knows, when the patient's history comes out, via the same psychiatrist, history that will neatly explain the new murder."

Julian stood immobile, silent, transfixed.

"Maybe it was even more direct than that," Edwards ruminated. "Maybe it was simple blackmail, after Hill's confession to him. Make him commit a second murder, in exchange for keeping quiet about the first. There's a pretty picture for you, huh?"

"But, I mean   it was so brutal!" Julian finally broke in.

"Tibor's directive. 'Make it look like a homicidal maniac. And not a lover scorned,' " said Edwards.

"Tibor *couldn't*! He's a *psychiatrist*!" Julian looked at Winston. "It's so . . . *far-fetched*."

"Only a possibility," Edwards said. "After all, only a possibility." He reached for the phone. "But in any case, it's time we make our own appointment to see the good Doctor, don't you think?"

In a moment, he was on with the nurse again. "Yes, as it turns out, we need to see him on some police business. Any time on that well-kept schedule tomorrow morning? Eleven o'clock? Good. Perfect. See you then."

THIRTY-NINE

They sat at dinner once again. Winston, Estelle, Julian.

She could feel, palpably, a new mood growing, rising fragrantly like the aroma from the kitchen, wafting through the heavy door into the tiny dining room. It seemed remarkable to her that this cramped claw-footed table, this odd, eccentric rococo wallpaper, could begin again to feel secure, alive; begin again to offer a sense of belonging, of home.

She recognized the scent: It was the scent of the trail. It was the smell, the taste, the aroma, of being closer, closer, to knowing.

Edwards must have sensed it too. He ate heartily, though silently. There was no dinner discussion of the case, out of either some long-held ethic or simply a long-established and respected pattern of

the Edwardses' dinner table, it seemed. But when
Estelle rose, toward the end of the meal, to clear
the dishes, he obviously could no longer suppress
it. He cocked his head, and spoke as if he and
Julian were in mid-discussion, correctly recogniz-
ing that they'd both been thinking of little else.

"You know, with his alibi coming from Dr.
Tibor, I never even considered Hill," Edwards confessed.

"I did," Julian reminded him curtly; her pride,
her aliveness unhidden.

"I know," admitted Edwards now. "And once
I charged Green," he said uncomfortably, "all Tibor had to do was give Hill an alibi. No assisting
the investigation, testifying, none of that."

"Pretty easy for a shrink to give a patient an
alibi."

"Tibor knowing all the time that if it doesn't
stick with Green, he can turn over Hill for it." Edwards paused, added reflectively, "Justify it to himself, maybe, by knowing the man's a killer
already."

Pure theory. Pure conjecture. "I don't
know . . ." she said.

"Hey, I don't, either," grumbled Edwards.
"That's why we're goin' to see him."

Forty-six stab wounds. She thought once more
of the pictures, the pictures that would not leave

her mind. "Forty-six stab wounds. That's rage, insanity, not a calculating assassin," she proposed once more.

Edwards glanced at Estelle.

Estelle turned away.

A quick, small moment.

Julian happened to see it.

"Well, better get some sleep," Edwards said then. "Six A.M. start, to see the doc upstate tomorrow morning. Gone 'fore you're up, Stelly."

Edwards and Julian rose to help clear the rest of the dinner table, shepherding the last of the plates and glasses into the kitchen.

"Like a little something to take out to the barn with you?" offered Estelle, eager, sincere, forlorn somehow. "Cinammon cookies?" she asked hopefully. "Some fruit?"

Always with the food. But one of Estelle's little goodies would be terrific just now. Julian smiled. "Sure am gonna miss all this good cooking when I'm gone. . . ."

The huge woman scurried to the breadbox for the cookies, gathered up some apples and pears, went over to the knife rack to slice them up for Julian.

Julian glanced at the orderly knife rack.

And saw that again, the knife was missing.

The serrated eight-inch knife. Absent once more.

Her heart leaped. Her mind raced. The kitchen swirled. Julian squinted to keep her balance, gripped a countertop to stay standing, to think. . . .

Angling to see. . . .

"You don't have to go through all the trouble of cutting that up," she managed to say.

"Oh, that's all right," said Estelle.

"Well, at least let me help you clean up. Here, let me get that for you."

She took the peels to the trash, the plate to the dishwasher.

Opened the dishwasher.

There were dishes.

Another knife with an obviously different handle.

But the eight-inch serrated one wasn't there.

FORTY

Julian sat on the edge of the bed in the barn apartment.

The room spun.

She gripped the bedframe.

Again the words and phrases played relentlessly in her head.

"Well, it was obviously a conversation you didn't hear. . . ."

"I wanted to see how he held the knife, that's all. . . ."

"I've got the sense the murderer is among us. . . ."

And loudest of all:

"Six A.M. start . . . Gone 'fore you're up, Stelly."

So no one would miss her. If she suddenly, simply, wasn't there.

And if anyone, any of his lackeys, was aware enough to even think of it or brazen enough to ask, Edwards would no doubt have some ready answer. *Oh, well, she's gone back to the big city. Didn't much like our way of life.*

Absent. Mark me absent. And simply, they would.

Realizations came rushing at her, bansheelike. Swarmed her, strafed her, in a firestorm of image and word and fact. . . .

"Think, now. When I was on the phone with Tibor in the next office, trying to figure out who the hell Green really was . . .," Edwards had said.

But Edwards had been in the next office when talking to Tibor. So she couldn't know—couldn't be sure—*what* had been said.

"Make it look like a homicidal maniac. And not a lover scorned. . . ." Couldn't even be sure, she realized now, that it had been Tibor on the other end.

And at that moment, the strained glance she'd caught between Edwards and Estelle . . . Just the unspoken tension of their marriage? Or unspoken acknowledgment of events to come?

Oh God.

It all began to arrange itself, to coalesce in her mind. . . .

He'd had to let Green off the hook, based on her evidence.

And with Green gone, he'd had to move quickly to keep her from turning her scrutiny to him again.

So he'd concocted this tale of Tibor and Sarah. Of some twisted psychological pact between Tibor and Green. So outrageous, so completely outrageous and elaborate, she had to believe it.

Dr. Tibor, she suddenly realized, had never slept with Sarah Langley. Had done so only in Edwards' vivid, calculating, efficient imagination.

Who knew what version of events he would give the rest of them, his dupes of thirty years. . . .

Had he actually concocted it all out of whole cloth? Was it possible? Was it actually possible?

Because the damn knife was gone from the rack again.

Swarming, strafing, a firestorm of image, word, and fact. . . .

Had Edwards created the elaborate story to protect Estelle? To stay one step ahead of Julian?

Or did it get even simpler than that?

"He was sleeping with that girl. I just know, that's all. . . ."

Was Estelle's pain and turmoil on that night for the reason Julian had first imagined?

Out of complexity, simplicity.

She took the jade necklace out of her pocket, looked at it closely. The clasp was broken cleanly off. The jade necklace Green said he'd given Sarah, that he'd picked up as he'd followed them through the woods.

Jade necklace. Blue scarf. White shoes. Ceiling fans and metal files. A psychic. A Perfect Crime. So ridiculous. All so ridiculous.

Green hadn't seen Edwards that night in the woods. But he *had* found the necklace. This necklace that Edwards never acknowledged when Julian mentioned it. Why not? *A gift,* she thought now. A gift from Green to Sarah. Was it the gift that had revealed to Edwards the existence of another man? That had unleashed his jealous fury?

Nausea rising, she saw the logic clearly now: She had mentioned the necklace to Edwards. It hadn't turned up with anyone or anywhere since. He would therefore know she had it.

His last loose end.

Christ.

She looked at the necklace. What would she have found on it? The fingerprints of Winston Edwards, from ripping it off Sarah's neck? *"Jealousy. Awfully ancient motive."* Her own words came back to her. Why hadn't she paid more attention? Why hadn't she counted it more? If she could just take the necklace now, have it dusted for prints . . .

Why hadn't she figured out the necklace?

Why hadn't she counted it more?

Some compulsion, some unconscious need to repeat? To repeat the pattern? To keep a crime "unsolved"?

That brutal night so long ago:

The sheriff, holding the knife in the doorway.

The nightie.

The man's laughter.

Frozen. Immobilized.

Reliving it now.

For the chance to change it?

Or to repeat it?

To become . . .

herself . . .

Unsolved?

She heard the footsteps on the path. Running.

Her heart skipped and began to race.

She looked up. It was a full-moon night. The kind that Green, as Hill, had correctly conjectured. Where black shoes could appear as white. Where you could see a lot.

And so she saw the figure.

The huge, hulking figure. But now there was no mistaking it. It wasn't Estelle. It wasn't Dr. Tibor. It wasn't the real Wayne Hill. It was the huge, hulking figure of Winston Edwards.

Running alarmingly fast, alarmingly energetically, toward the barn and toward her.

And something was in his hand, she could see. Something held tightly, half hidden in his massive bear-paw hand, but as bright and glistening in Julian's mind at that moment as in the mind of a psychic.

The emotional turmoil, the chaos of thought and feeling inside her, permitted her for that intensive moment to somehow see the knife in his hand. Clear, bright, shining. *This is what a psychic sees,* she thought briefly. A fleeting moment of connection with genuine psychic ability. A strange vividness beyond intuition. A brief psychic moment— and a good chance the remarkable moment would be one of her last.

She had been wrong. She had let down her guard. And now, tonight, in the Edwardses' barn apartment, she was going to pay.

"No phone, I'm afraid. Took it out when the kids left . . ."

She had just seconds before he bounded up the steps.

She scooped the necklace back into her pocket.

She stuffed pillows beneath the bedsheets, to make the bed look occupied.

Please God.

She got behind the door.

She could only hope to surprise him.

She turned off the light.

She held her breath.

The familiar nausea rose again.

She waited.

Outside, it was silent.

He was casing it.

She saw his glasses, his nose, loom through the window to the far side.

Then, in a moment, through the other window.

She stood still behind the door.

The door handle turned.

The door opened slowly.

She stood behind it.

Winston Edwards opened the door slowly, very slowly, while looking at the bed, and thus had the opportunity to see a knife—a knife his young assistant, thinking quickly, had taken from the dishwasher just a short while ago—a knife now held up to the side of his face by his young assistant, standing behind the door.

His huge eyes widened, alarmed, behind his wire-rimmed glasses. "Julian."

"Winston," she said evenly.

"I . . . I didn't want to wake you."

"As you can see, you didn't," she said, still evenly.

At least he knows it won't be without a fight.

Some reserve of strength—fueled by rage—was keeping her from shaking, was keeping the knife steady and true.

He turned very slowly toward her, his eye on her knife. "I came to tell you . . ."

Julian now glanced down at Winston Edwards' hands.

There was no knife in either one.

He was gripping a map.

Rolled up tightly in his hand.

Crumpled at one end. Glossy white.

Reflective in the moonlight.

"I . . . I just had a call from Zimmern Upstate," Edwards said. "It's Tibor. He's dead. And Hill's disappeared. We've got to get up there. Now."

Julian slowly lowered her knife.

The wind wailed.

"Meet you in front in five minutes," he instructed.

FORTY-ONE

Julian and Edwards drove silently north.

The headlights' dim parabola grazed and slithered across the bare-branched trees to either side, hungrily licked at the sameness of road ahead of them.

Clouds had gathered thick and fast above them, making the night turn starless. Moonless. Wind-whipped. Bitter cold.

Julian noticed a manila envelope on the car seat between them.

The old Impala seemed to strain mightily against the wind and night, and yet was steady, unshakable, determined.

"I figure it this way," said Edwards, breaking the silence inside the car. "Tibor's nurse at some point mentioned our call about vacation travel to the good doctor. Next thing he knows, we've got an appointment to see him. No problem for Tibor. He'll give up Hill, like he planned all along. Problem is, Hill *also* knows we're coming to see Tibor. Somehow's found out about our appointment, probably through the same nurse. And it's obvious to Hill that if we start pushin' Tibor, he'll give Hill up. So Hill confronts Tibor. Having just had his refresher course in killing. And here we are."

"So we've issued an APB on Hill?"

"No," Edwards said. "I didn't want everyone out here stumbling all over each other."

Or you couldn't bear the thought of not being the hero yourself.

Julian felt the frustration, the rage at his backwardness, his stubbornness, his pride, rising again in her. She could not contain it. "But . . . I don't understand. . . . How can we possibly expect to find Wayne Hill in a thousand square miles, if it's just us?"

Edwards smiled. "For me, Julian, this is the easy part," he said. "The part where I'm comfortable. Some people around here get all hushed and reverent about Winston Edwards' skills, and you know well as I do, for the most part it's all a lot of talk. But this might be the part where they're right."

He looked at the road, drove calmly through the dark. "For me, this has *always* been the easy part. I've always been able to just . . . think like them."

Julian shifted uncomfortably.

"Besides," said Edwards, "we're finally getting a break. Look around you, Miz Palmer. Think. What do you see?"

Julian squinted through the windshield into the dark.

What was he talking about?

Darkness.

Woods.

Then she saw. Visible for the moment, only in the glow of the headlights.

Of course.

"I didn't want everyone out here stumbling all over each other."

Snow.

Fresh snow.

"It's the Snow Belt, Miz Palmer," said Edwards affectionately. "Snow pilin' up fast, and nobody else out here." He smiled. His gimlet eyes shone in the dark. "Be like trackin' an animal."

The snow. Of course.

This late at night, no one on the road, except the one set of tracks. One set of tracks to follow.

The Snow Belt.

The snow she had never seen. The snow that had lured her in the first place. The snow she had thought about, vaguely, whimsically, that day in the police counselor's office.

A way of covering, of forgetting.

And here, it was uncovering. Here, it was a path to solving.

She watched it tumble sparkling through the headlights.

Saw it begin to silently accumulate at the side of the road.

The snow. Not covering. But *un*covering.

Its meaning for her had changed entirely.

But she'd been right, at least, that it would have meaning.

Had it been her intuition? A sixth sense about it?

In the dark of the car, she smiled.

Suddenly there was an upcountry gas station. A beacon in the night. Approaching it, its lit sign stood in absurd modern contrast to its dirty and ramshackle building.

Just as suddenly they pulled into it. Edwards reached for the manila envelope between them.

He pulled out of it a copy of the newspaper article that Richards had sent. Julian watched as Edwards creased and folded it so all that showed was the photo of Wayne Hill.

He looked up at her. "Only known photograph," he said. "Wait here." And before she could protest, he was out of the car and she was watching through the gas station's paned-glass window as he showed the photograph to the clerk.

She could see the clerk say something to Edwards, and point up the road.

Edwards came lurching out of the gas station, and pointed up the road to Julian.

"Someone's on the run, the one thing he thinks straight about is gas," he said, after a while, when they were under way again. "Needs a full tank. And that's the only place open."

He was teaching her, after all. Maybe not teaching, exactly, not lecturing, or holding forth, as he had in the past, but simply letting her see, for whatever it was worth to her, his own thinking, his own mental processes. Simply verbalizing his relevant thoughts.

Maybe, maybe after all this, this hellish internship was going to be somehow worth something.

"He won't try to cross the Canadian border," said Edwards quietly. "He'll figure we put out an APB, and that they'll be looking for him. It's the middle of the night. He hasn't got many options. Hotels and motels are out, because we'll check those, and even if he hides his vehicle and uses another name, he knows we can narrow it down to late check-ins. Summer, he'd camp. Winter, he'll look to go inside somewhere. A cabin. And with that quick takeoff from the hospital, he'll need to look for supplies. Or sleep in his car."

The snow began to fall in earnest now. Somehow its silent accumulation crossed into forcefulness, becoming powerful, altering, reckonable.

Edwards turned off the highway and headed up a country road for a mile or so, to pull into a small market. Its windows were brightly lit.

"This place stays open to take night deliveries, because of the truck routes and timing," he said. "Only place I know around here that does. And one of those strange places everyone knows." He grabbed the folded photo from beside him again. "Stay here. Back in a flash."

"No. This time I go with you," she said.

"It's freezing cold. I'll be right back," he smiled paternally.

"Hey, I'm not waiting in the car," she said firmly.

He shrugged. "Suit yourself."

The wind and snow assaulted her, and then she was inside the bright market.

Edwards approached the clerk at the counter. Looked at him. Loomed over him. "Edwards. Canaanville Police." The clerk stared back without response. Edwards took out the photograph of Hill from beneath his coat, held it up to the man's nose challengingly, imperiously. "Seen him?"

The man nodded a quick yes.

"Bought some things, did he?"

The man nodded again.

"And . . . ?"

"Well, he, uh . . ." And the clerk pointed vaguely out the plate-glass window and up the road.

Before the clerk even looked back to Edwards, the Bear was out the door, Julian right behind him.

He trotted to the car a few steps ahead of her, and even in the fierce wind, she saw the huge man's trot was limber, lithe, alive.

The huge man who not hours before had come trotting down that path, she'd thought, to kill her.

But now she could see that the trot, the aliveness, the eagerness, the purpose in his step and the light in his eyes, were from being on the trail of a killer. Being on the path to a solution.

And his not wanting her to come in with him, she saw, seemed to be nothing more than old-fashioned, misplaced chivalry. Not wanting her to get whipped and soaked by the wind and snow. It was the Winston Edwards who still didn't believe that women belonged in police work. The Winston Edwards held back in time. She shook her head; she smiled. They jumped back into the car. Grinning almost childlike, he eagerly put the Impala into gear, and pointed it up the road.

"Your instincts are . . . amazing," she admitted to the car cabin's dark, when they had driven in silence a while longer.

And suddenly, out of her own instinct, something came to her, and she felt comfortable enough, and felt he would be too, here in the warm dark, for her to pose it aloud. "That's why you hired a psychic, isn't it?" she said quietly. " 'Cause you recognized something in it?" It began to fall together, to make more sense. "And that's why we went all the way to Raleigh-Durham," she said, realizing. "You weren't all that curious about Wayne Hill. You were curious about yourself."

She remembered his interest on the tour. Silently soaking it all in.

"Psychic." Edwards said the word aloud, alone, let it hang in the air, as if to hear how it sounded. To examine for a moment, its letters, its shape. "Might just be a fancy word for 'instinct.' A high degree of it. So much instinct it starts to feel funny. . . ." he said. He frowned uncomfortably. Pressed his lips together. And Julian could tell it was something that made him nervous, that he didn't want to look at too closely.

His stunning abilities that first day.

Her briefcase. Her suit. Her haircut. Her preinterview activities.

His instincts that night in Raleigh-Durham. Half knowing about her upbringing. Her town. Her family. Her father. By her posture. By the look in her eyes. By trusting in his own sense of it.

His putting-together—his intuiting—the possibilities of Tibor. Of Hill. Of their relationship. And look—now Tibor was dead and Hill had run, in a confirmation of those intuitions and suspicions.

His no-less-stunning tracking abilities tonight.

But he had held Green, against the evidence. He had been intent on solving it no matter what— against the evidence if need be. He had laughingly presented the idea of his own vanity as the reason. Laughingly presented, Julian saw now, to disguise the fact, to make somehow palatable, that that *was* the reason.

Why? Why was someone so capable, so provincial? Why was someone so talented, so destructive?

Somehow, there in the dark of the Impala, she felt she understood.

Because, while he was amazing, he was also human. Had his incredible, natural, God-given talents and instincts, and his natural, God-given shortcomings and foibles, too. He was human.

And she thought again of Sarah Langley. The high-school photograph of Sarah Langley, that Edwards had carried. His easy familiarity with her apartment. His quick, pained looking-away, when he brought up the potential of Sarah Langley's duplicity.

The cabin of the car was warm, secure. They drove in silence. It was time to know the truth.

"Chief . . . ?"

She let the inquisitive tone hang in the cabin a moment, gave him a chance to prepare himself, to ready himself, for what he must know was coming.

"Chief, Sarah Langley . . ."

She let that name, too, hang in the thick cabin air, unhurried, waiting.

"Sarah Langley," the Chief said back in a moment, with uncharacteristic quiet, calm, as if he had come to some new understanding of the name, some new, deeper recognition of it.

For a moment she thought that there would be no more forthcoming from him. And then, in the dark, he began to speak.

"It's what you think, Julian," said Edwards. "It's exactly what you think. An old man in a loveless marriage. An old man with a good dose of vanity, used to a healthy measure of local respect and power. An old man fast comin' to the end of the only life he ever knew. The only satisfaction he ever knew. The world, the love, of his job. Soon to give it up. Feelin' a little fragile, a little lost. A young, pretty, single cocktail waitress, a wild girl. No strings attached. It's just what you think, Julian."

He drove on. "We saw each other, I don't know, thirty times over the year. Estelle knew I was goin' somewhere. I didn't want to hurt her. But I'm sure I did."

They drove on in silence, before Julian asked, "Did you love her?"

He was silent.

"Did you?"

Edwards squinted his eyes. "It's a cold country, Julian," he said. "It's a long winter. It's a hard life. Did I love her?" He shrugged. "What exactly is love, anyway? That's somethin' my famous intuition fails me on."

Julian watched the snow, accumulating now at the sides of the road.

"Guess you can amend your view now," said Edwards gruffly. "From 'old man,' to 'foolish old man.' " He paused. "But I tell you this," he said. "She was somethin'." He shook his head in amazement. "She was somethin'."

Had it ever occurred to him, she wondered, that maybe he'd been holding Green purely out of jealousy? *"Jealousy. Awfully ancient motive."* Their earlier discussion came back to her.

But then another motive occurred to her—larger, more fitting and complete. And carefully, respectfully, gently, quietly, she pointed it out.

"No wonder you were holding Green. No wonder you were so irrationally bent on getting him for it. You couldn't retire without solving her murder. You simply . . . couldn't."

Edwards smiled. "You're smart, Julian. Real smart. Like I said, you can probably do anything in this world you want. Remember I asked you once, at that dinner—for someone so smart, someone who could do anything, why on earth would you choose police work? Well I'll confess now," he nodded slightly, proudly, approvingly, "I'm glad you did."

For Julian, that little nod filled the warm cabin of the old Impala, and they drove on in silence.

She felt foolish for having doubted him. If only she had spent this kind of time with him, if only he had confided in her before, not pushed her away, if only he had included her more, let her in on more, not planted her at the metal desk outside his office and outside his trust. Then she would have believed in him. She *wouldn't* have doubted him.

And as for her own psychic moment? Picturing the glistening knife as he ran down the path toward her? *Hah!* What she'd thought was a knife had turned out to be a map. From an object of nightmare, of doom, to . . . What? What was a map? Perspective. A way to see more. In a glimpse, to have the world open before you. . . .

She knew she would never have the abilities of a Winston Edwards. Not by a long shot. But her instincts were developing. Her instincts were coming along. And as they drove closer to some ultimate comprehension of the last night of Sarah Langley, she felt again drawn closer to the highly talented Chief.

The snow was coming even heavier now. The white silent blanket steadily thickening. No longer a beautiful, glistening coating, but rather, fresh and relentless evidence of nature's weight and might; a fresh reminder of nature's ruling hand.

A huge snowplow came groaning and roaring

past from the opposite direction, its yellow lights flashing, then lumbering off down the road behind them.

Wouldn't that take away any tire tracks? thought Julian.

She looked at Edwards.

But Edwards seemed unconcerned, or not to notice. He was already focused elsewhere.

"There's only two parks with campgrounds big enough to hide out in," he said. "He grew up here. Knows how to fish and hunt. He's done enough police work to know that if you can lie low even for a little while, your odds of escape get much better."

He squinted out at the road. "This here Route Four is always the first road plowed. Only road we can't see his tracks on. Only road he'd even have a chance on. And it eventually hits those campsites. . . ."

Amazing.

"Good Christ!" shouted Edwards suddenly.

He stepped hard on the brakes.

The old Impala swerved, fishtailed mildly, and came to a halt.

"What?!"

Fiercely Edwards backed the car up about a hundred feet. He furiously turned the wheel, angled the car, to train the headlights on the side of the road.

"Huh," he said.

There, illuminated in the headlights, was a set of tire tracks. Veering off the road, and into the woods.

They both stared for a moment, until Julian asked, "How the hell did you see them?"

"Simple," said Winston Edwards. "I was lookin' for 'em."

"But you just said the campground . . ."

"Well he *knows* I'm thinkin' 'bout those campgrounds," said Edwards, as if it were the most obvious thing in the world.

I'm learning. Really learning. Learning at last, she thought, fear and pulse and excitement all rising equally in her, as he turned the car into the edge of the woods, found low gear, and headed in.

While the snow was coming fast now, it did not yet cover the telltale tire tracks ahead of them. The old Impala bounced, bounded, and struggled over the slippery, hard frozen ground. Unpausing, unflinching, expressionless, 260 pounds hunched into pure focus, Winston the Bear Edwards followed the tracks without looking elsewhere even for a moment. Julian vaguely wondered how they would ever get the car out, but clearly that did not seem to be on Edwards' mind. In fact, it seemed to Julian to be the one thing he hadn't thought about. But she might turn out to be wrong about that, too.

In the headlights, in a minute or so, the tracks became suddenly unclear. Crisscrossed. Confusing.

Edwards' brow furrowed.

The car slowed and stopped.

He sat for a moment, regarding the crisscrossing tracks. Then suddenly—impulsively, explosively—the car turned left.

There, suddenly visible in the headlights . . .

. . . like a deer frozen in terror . . .

. . . was the tall, gangly, awkward man from the newspaper photograph.

As if that old and faded black-and-white newspaper photograph—the only known photo, the one she had twice breathlessly brought into Winston Edwards' office, the photograph now folded on the seat between them—

—as if it had come eerily alive.

There in the white glow of the headlights, was the real Wayne Hill.

And just as she focused on the famous right hand—the four fingers, the missing fifth, utterly clear in the headlights' glare—Wayne Hill turned and took off into the woods.

The hulking form of Winston Edwards was

somehow out of the car only a heartbeat later, taking off after him.

Julian was right behind him.

Out of the headlights' penetrating beams, the dark grew intense.

The snow fell harder.

Edwards and Julian stumbled through the woods in an adrenaline rush, struggling brazenly for breath, the frozen leaves and twigs crackling loudly under them, the cold and wet coating them, snapping at them, the night swallowing them, they chased him.

The woods. The moonlight. The beat of breath. The chase. Even in the midst of it, the eerie similarity, the echo of Sarah Langley's last moments, was not lost on Julian, and made its way, insinuated itself, into some calm corner of her brain.

The woods suddenly opened onto a snowy field, where Julian caught her first glimpse of Wayne Hill since the moment in the headlights.

"Stop!" Edwards shouted hoarsely.

Julian saw Edwards reach inside his coat and pull out a gun. A semiautomatic pistol of some sort, she could tell by its outline. She'd never seen him carry a weapon before.

Hill continued across the frozen field.

He had reached its far edge, and was about to enter the woods on the other side when he tripped and fell into the snow.

In a moment, Edwards and Julian were over him.

All three breathless. Panting. Staring at one another.

The weapon dangled from Edwards' right hand. A 9-millimeter Beretta, Julian could see now. A long way from departmental standard issue, she knew.

Hill put up his arms in vague defense.

"You killed him!" Edwards screamed, rage uncontained, unleashed.

Hill looked desperate, confused. "No, no! Why? . . . Why are you *saying* this? . . . Why are you *doing* this? . . ." He looked to Edwards, to Julian, to Edwards, a trapped animal.

"You killed him!" Edwards screamed again, identically, incantatory.

"No! . . . No! . . . Please!" Hill looked at Julian now. "Look, I just . . . just want to . . ." Rolling a shoulder out of the snow, beginning to struggle up . . .

Edwards fired point-blank at Hill and hit him squarely in the forehead.

Hill collapsed instantly back into the snow.

A cherry of blood swelled neatly from his forehead, then forged a path down the left side of his face.

"Oh my God!" said Julian.

The woods spun around her.

"How . . . how could you . . ."

"I was threatened," Edwards said calmly.

"Threatened!"

"He had a knife."

From his coat pocket, Edwards pulled out a knife in a plastic bag.

He took the knife out of the bag.

"A serrated eight-inch knife," observed Edwards.

He bent down heavily, slowly, methodically, and placed the knife in Hill's right hand, carefully wrapping Hill's fingers around it. "Ordinary kitchen knife. Hill's MO, I guess, these kinds of knives."

"You killed Tibor!" Julian said, the panic rising in a tide.

Edwards smiled. "Tibor isn't dead," he said, shaking his head. "That's just something I told you. Like I told Hill. Told him the Great Chief Edwards knew he did it, and the Great Chief Edwards would get him for it." Edward stood up now, straightened, looked suddenly huge in the moonlight reflected in the white snow. "That set him running, didn't it? Sometimes I do rely on the myth, I guess. . . ."

Julian's mind raced. It careened useless, chaotic, bumping up against itself, the wealth of evidence crashing into more evidence, all of it flying directionless, suspended, around her mind . . .

"But . . . the airline tickets," she said, reeling. "Tibor leaving a day later . . ."

"Did you actually *see* what was on the paper Simms handed me?" Edwards asked. " 'Depart October eighth,' " he mimed cynically. "That's just something I said. Always check the evidence, Julian. Always check the evidence."

Julian felt herself backing up slowly, felt herself slowly realizing. "Oh my God," she said. "You . . . you *did* make it all up . . . to get me up here . . . in the woods . . ."

Edwards leveled the gun at her. "Give me the necklace, Julian."

Julian kept backing up.

"The necklace," she repeated, abstractly, unthinking, unable to.

"The one I gave Sarah."

"The last piece of evidence," said Julian, dazed.

She took it out of her pocket, dangled it in her hand.

The sight of it steadied her a little. Brought her back a little, somehow. A fact. Not floating talk. Not theory. A necklace. Made of jade. A mineral.

A rock. Tangible. Factual. Here in her hand.

And out of the same pocket she drew the other piece of evidence she still had there, that in some profound way she knew, she felt, went with the necklace.

The high-school photo of Sarah Langley.

"Evidence," Green, as Tibor, had said, handing it to her that day.

"Still got your photo," she said slowly, carefully. "Sarah Langley. A person. A life."

She tossed the photograph toward Edwards.

It caught in the wind.

It floated . . . tumbled . . .

And landed several yards off in the snow.

Edwards looked momentarily, automatically, impulsively, to where it landed.

And when he did, Julian turned and ran.

He turned back a moment later. Lifted the gun.

Paused.

Only a moment.

Then fired.

Missed.

Took off after Julian.

*   *   *

She leaped and stumbled through the snow.

Sarah . . . Sarah . . .

Felt the beast, relentless, huffing, puffing, stumbling behind her.

Think. Don't think. Stop. Don't stop. A jumble. All logic, all power, self, everything, collapsed. . . .

Behind her, a gun firing. . . .

Bullets bouncing off a tree fiercely, like fiery creatures disturbed.

Julian ran.

Faster.

Faster.

Looked behind her, just for a moment, to see . . .

What!

No!

She screams.

Then there is silence.

Heart pounding, struggling for breath, the Bear stumbles through the crunching snow, and suddenly stops.

Before him is an embankment. Gun drawn, he regards it. Approaches it cautiously.

Looks carefully over it.

A ravine.

A hundred-foot drop to an icy stream.

Dizzying. Sudden.

And there, far below, barely discernible through the black night and falling snow, but visible enough, he sees the dark coat, dark against the white collecting snow.

He waits. Silent. Still.

There is no movement.

He puts away the gun.

He steps carefully away from the embankment, as if respectfully away from a tomb.

Check the evidence. Always check the evidence.

He steps forward again.

Takes out the gun.

He braces. Aims steadily, carefully . . .

Pulls the trigger.

The shot resounds through the woods.

He can see the black coat jump; the body in the black coat jumps by the icy stream.

He fires again.

The coat jumps again.

Eyes narrowed against the wind and snow, he squints into the ravine . . .

And happens to see it. Or thinks he can. Barely perceptible. Reflective in the snow. A glint of green, by the black coat. The jade necklace.

He steps back from the precipice.

Tucks the gun under his coat.

Turns, and heads back through the woods toward the body of Wayne Hill, and toward the car.

He turns back only once, to see that the snow, falling heavy, leaden, silent, is already covering his tracks.

He regards for a moment the body of Wayne Hill. The hands by his head. The four-fingered hand pointed, ironically, in the direction of the embankment.

He smiles, heads for the car.

From the passenger side, he opens the glove compartment. Turns on the police radio. Punches in the numbers.

The cherry police lights spun in the pale pink dawn.

Chief Richards—tall, lean, angular, stooped, pale, floating in his trench coat—blew his breath against his hands, stamped his feet to stay warm.

"You shoulda called for backup."

Edwards shrugged.

Richie smiled affectionately, shook his head. " 'Course, you never would."

Edwards looked at him sheepishly, sharing his amusement.

Edwards and Richards looked once more at the snowy imprint of Hill's body, now photographed, removed, and under a police tarpaulin.

"He went for me," said Edwards, an afterthought.

"So it was Hill, after all. . . ." Chief Richards said to his old friend.

Edwards nodded soberly.

"Huh," said Richards, surprised, and not surprised at all.

One of Richards' officers brought the Impala back out to the road, and checked it over cursorily. Chief Richards and Chief Edwards stood by the side of the road watching him, day slowly gathering around them.

The snow had ended—looked to be just about six inches or so this time. Everything white and pristine. The sky had cleared to a crisp, crystalline, dazzling blue.

"Still runs, I guess," observed Richards, as they walked toward the old Impala.

"Nothing can kill it," said Edwards proudly.

He tugged open the heavy blue door, laboriously lowered himself in.

"Say, whatever happened to that young intern of yours? One I joked with on the phone."

"Julian?"

"Was that her name? Huh."

"Went back to the big city. Internship was over."

"Too bad she couldn't see how it ended up, I guess."

"Yeah. Too bad," said Edwards.

"Think she learned anything? I mean, this whole damn internship thing . . ."

"Oh, she was real smart, that one. I think she learned about all she could."

Edwards thrust his hand out the window to Chief Richards. "Thanks for comin' out here to get me."

"Don't be silly."

"See you soon."

Unsolved.

 Unsolved.

 Her own life.

 Her own death.

 Unsolved.

FORTY-TWO

Winston Edwards' retirement party was precisely the raucous, classless affair that all its participants had fervently hoped for. It was held in the social hall of the Methodist church, and the invitees looked forward to desecrating by night's end any holiness extant in the site when the evening began.

Up here, they called the season winter, although by the calendar it was still technically the fall. They called it winter in recognition, in brooding anticipation, in resignation, to the local reality.

And so far, it had been a season harder than usual, preoccupied with murder, a winter already bleaker than normal, even before settling its blanket of white silence onto the landscape and insinuating its cold into the inhabitants' bones.

But now the snow covered it in white—would continue to now, reliably, repeatedly, throughout

the next months. Now the snow covered over what
had been exposed and laid bare—shortcomings,
foibles, failures, and flaws of mind and spirit as
well as of landscape—and now, with the snow, it
was all on hold, suspended, unjudged.

And now a murder was solved, the murder of
a young waitress. So this was a celebration not
only of Winston Edwards' retirement, but of murder no longer hanging over Canaanville, of a case
no longer hanging over the Canaanville police, and
of winter itself—cleansing, disguising, sterilizing,
serene. Of course, there were plenty here who were
celebrating not Winston Edwards so much as Winston Edwards' stepping down. For them, that was
greatest celebration of all.

The room was festooned with disposable dec-
oration. Rock music blared distorted and incomprehensible from an ancient hi-fi system, its tubes
fiercely aglow, its loudspeakers trembling. As if
there was music only to say there had been, and to
keep from hearing one another too well. Unlikely
couples formed to dance, under paper-thin guises
of graciousness, civility, spontaneity, and innocent
fun.

Hand-scrawled banners suspended on string
spanned the corners of the room. "The Bear Finally
Hibernates." "Forty Years in the Dessert. (Ha-ha.)
Congratulations."

Estelle Edwards seemed to have raided a dozen attics for her get-up. She was fortified in jewelry. It was her single night in thirty years to dress up, and she clearly had little experience with it.

Dinner was southern barbecue prepared by Herman, the Rhine Brothers cook, on a huge grill set up outside, where guests watched through the window as the poor man froze.

In his best suit and tie, the pale, angular Chief Richards looked lugubrious and out of place. Like a mortician, or the uncomfortable minister at a wedding reception. But of course, he couldn't—he wouldn't—have missed this party for the world.

His old friend, Winston Edwards.

He found himself finally standing next to Winston at one point, and shouted to be heard above the din of the music.

"Hey, I'm surprised your intern didn't come up for your retirement party," he called into Edwards' cocked ear.

"She was invited," Edwards shouted back. "No response. Guess the big-city girl don't want anything to do with upcountry anymore."

Richards nodded knowing assent.

The music was turned off the moment the barbecue was set out, on ten identical round tables. Ten or so guests arranged themselves matter-of-factly at each table, and as they munched and continued drinking, silent and contented, someone switched on the microphone on the small stage that occupied one side of the hall, and the "speechifying" began.

It was drunken and rambling, like the sloppy send-off sentiments expressed at a bachelor party. A painful parade of station-house irregulars and Canaanville denizens seemed compelled to take the stage, some muttering incomprehensibly or giggling with embarrassment once there, others proudly and ceaselessly inflicting irreparable damage on the English language. Eventually, Mayor Yates made his way to the microphone, indicating to all a finale to the grim cavalcade. His speech needed to be only marginally more coherent and eloquent than the previous ones to soar in comparison.

"Winston the Bear Edwards. The bear of a man we've had to bear thirty years in these parts. The investigative genius who never left us. Fifty-five homicides across this North Country, every one solved." He paused to let the two astonishing facts sink in. The violent loss of life over so many years. And the matching record of justice, of resolution, of rightness, tit for tat, year after year, decade after decade. "How will our police department survive without you?" The mayor seemed to straighten, to physically rise up proudly behind his rhetoric. "Well, we'll have to learn more, work harder, think faster." He paused, smiled slightly. "In short, we'll just have to . . . Bear Up."

Appreciative laughter. Approving applause. And it seemed clear that the "speechifying" was done, or that this was as good an ending as any, and that the evening would now start winding down.

But before anyone could get up, Chief Richards stood, waved his hand inquiringly at the mayor. "Mind if I say a little somethin'?"

The mayor smiled graciously, shrugged loosely. "Why sure," he said expansively. "Folks," he declared by way of introduction, "Chief Richards, over to Northward. One of Winston's oldest, closest friends."

Richards stepped unceremoniously onto the stage and up to the microphone.

He smiled at Edwards at the front table, made a modest deferential bow. "Winston the Bear Edwards," he said expansively, in an obvious, direct, and self-conscious echo of the mayor. "A man who for as long as I've known him, has always had his own way of doin' things. Catchin' a bass . . . or a criminal." Mild laughter. "Fact is, tonight, just to prove how much he does things his own way, we got somethin' special planned for him."

Richards could hear the murmur of interest in the audience. There hadn't been anything very special to the party so far.

"Hope this'll be as memorable for all of you as I expect it'll be for him. . . ."

Chief Richards paused for a moment, paused to fix on Edwards, to brace his own gaze, ready his police being, so as not to miss the next moment.

"Ladies and gentlemen," he said, "someone a few of you know. Winston Edwards' first and only intern. Miss Julian Palmer."

Silently, purposefully, she strode through a side door, stepped up onto the stage, and stood at the microphone for a moment, regarding the room, taking it in, before looking down at Edwards.

Chief Richards watched his old friend Edwards collapse back into his chair as if punched. He watched Edwards begin blinking, continue blinking, reflexively, autonomically, strangely, insanely. Edwards looked stricken. Aged. Winston the Bear Edwards. Cowering in the corner of a cave.

Anyone looking at that moment toward the stooped, thin Richards in his ill-fitting suit would have seen an expression mixing righteousness and sadness, melding victory and loss, all of them knit together grimly on the tall man's face. But no one saw it. Everyone was looking, understandably, at the radiant young woman onstage.

"Well," Julian began, slowly, deliberately, clearly, the first address from the dais that evening not drunken or slovenly or embarrassed, but clear, crisp, clean, "it certainly is a pleasant surprise for me to be here tonight. In fact," she said, looking at Edwards, "I feel lucky to be here at all."

Running . . .
   Falling . . .
   Running . . .
   God . . .
   Please . . .

Julian stumbles across the frozen field.

The snow is thick now, a wall of white as she runs, so thick she cannot really see.

Two shots ring out, puncture the air, sunder the universe. They thwack fiercely off trees to the side of her.

She turns to look behind her, an instinctive turn, a moment to assess. For a second, faced away from the snow and wind blinding her, she can actually see. . . .

She turns forward . . .

Feels her leg give way . . .

Tumbles forward into thin air . . .

Airborne . . .

Oh God . . .

Her hands, her being, open instantly to the shock.

The jade necklace leaves her hand.

Oh God . . .

The body covered by the tarp on the farmhouse floor . . .

The springs of her sister's bunk bed above her . . .

The sheriff in the doorway . . .

Vivid.

That is what comes to her.

That is all.

Her life's theme:

Unsolved . . .

Her life . . .

Her death . . .

Unsolved . . .

And then . . .

Ahhh!

A loud crunch.

A spray of white dust . . .

She is rolling . . .

She is stopped.

Covered in snow.

Her hip, her knees, her hands. The pain . . .

Branches, brambles . . .

Edwards . . .

In an instant, she orients herself. Looks up and sees a ledge about twenty feet above her . . .

Where I fell . . .

Edwards . . .

An outcropping of rock juts from the cliff just a few feet away from her . . .

She rolls under it . . .

Commands her breath to slow, to still . . .

Waits. . . .

Waits. . . .

She hears nothing.

Then two more shots puncture the night, sever the universe again.

I'm dead. . . .

But I'm alive.

But I'm dead.

She lies curled up . . .

Waits for the shot to find her.

Waits. . . .

Breath held for the end.

She wants to scream for it.

She wants to cry for it.

But she is too tired. Too terrified. Too far past them. . . .

She can only lie, curled, waiting, unmoving.

Waiting. . . .
No more shots are fired.

She waits some more.

Watches the snow fall.

And then, emerging somehow, emerging from instinct back to thought, she begins to feel the cold,
and the pain,
and knows, knows, that she must begin to move, or will die.

She is confused.

Doesn't understand.

She crawls out slowly, carefully, childlike from under the ledge.

Looks up.

Looks down.

Far down.

Sees a black coat, discernible through the snow.

A black coat. Like hers.

Oh my God.

A body.

In the streambed, a hundred feet below.

Good Christ.

Julian begins to understand. . . .

*   *   *

Bedraggled, exhausted—pants coat eyebrows hair caked with snow from scrambling and stumbling down the cliffside, grabbing limbs that sometimes held, sometimes released and sent her tumbling— Julian Palmer stands, panting, over the body in the streambed.

The coat on it is untorn. Like new. Its artificial fibers virtually unchanged by the elements. Same with the black rubber boots.

But the body inside them—what is left of it— that is a different story.

The wind rips relentlessly through the ravine. She notices how the wind lifts the powdery snow, brushes it from the body. Which is why, she thinks vaguely, the body remains exposed.

She checks her gloves, pulls them on tighter.

Reaches carefully out to it.

She turns it over.

She gags. Pauses. Calms herself. . . .

She looks at what remains of the body.

The unsolved murder upstate.

She can hear the theory again in her head. . . .

"What if Hill is seeing a psychiatrist to begin with, because of the guilt? —I mean, the loss-of-powers thing, that's just the public version of the story, let's say. Let's say he's seeing the shrink for a real reason—intolerable, soul-wrenching guilt. . . . 'Catch me, find me, end this ordeal.' "

And even speculating wildly, vamping it complexly to fool her, even then, it turned out, Edwards had been right.

No wonder poor Hill had chosen this stretch of woods. A dead body had remained undiscovered here, he knew. Why not his own live one, too?

Then she saw it—to the side of the body—half buried in the snow, but half showing.

A glint of green.

The necklace. The jade necklace.

She scooped up the necklace, dropped it into her pocket.

Backed away from the body.

Began the arduous climb out of the frozen ravine.

"Yes," she said graciously from the podium now. "Lucky to be here," she told them, "to help celebrate the end of Winston Edwards' remarkable career."

She smiled at him.

He sat frozen, immobilized, in the front row, in the place of honor.

At seven in the evening, in a neat Victorian home far in the north, a doorbell rings.

Chief Richards, on the evening of an enormously long and exhausting day that started at dawn, tending to a murder scene just off Route 4, is sitting down to a quiet dinner with his wife, and is loath to be interrupted for any reason.

Richards goes to the door, looks through the peephole, opens it.

Bedraggled, exhausted, breathing hard, an unkempt but somehow self-possessed young woman, of obvious decency and of equally obvious recent trouble, is standing there.

"I'm Julian Palmer. I need to speak to you."

He gestures her in, and even then—at some level, some level of instinct, before she has said a word—some odd things begin to gel, begin to fit together.

A quiet is settling over the assemblage. The clink of plates is lessening, the laughter is quelling, there is an attentiveness—as if, by Edwards' expression, by Richards', by Julian's, the celebrants are sensing that something is up. Something serious.

"See, it wasn't me down there in that icy stream, Winston," she says. "It was Hill's victim. And while you were just speculating about Hill trying to relieve the guilt, turns out you were right. All the weight of your wild accusation, all the fear it put into him, his lack of choices, look where he was leading us." She paused. Couldn't help but smile. "You solved another one. Your record's intact. So . . . congratulations."

There was an uncomfortable shifting and murmuring in the audience now. All were listening. Looking at Edwards. Who sat impassive. Immobile.

"But we're in the Snow Belt, Winston. The sun never reaches down into that ravine, the snow doesn't melt off till high summer, and the stream's icy year-round."

She regarded him meaningfully. There might as well have been no one else in the assembly hall. "See, up here, certain things can stay preserved. Undiscovered. Unseen. A long time."

She looked at him. "But not forever."

She raised her index finger, and delivered her lesson mildly. "Check the evidence, Winston," she reminded him gently. "Always check the evidence."

The room was still. The room was focused. Had ceased to be a loose, disorganized, splay-limped gathering of a hundred revelers; had become instead somehow a single set of eyes and ears, looking, listening, completely, intently.

"At dinner one night in Raleigh-Durham, you once mentioned the idea of someone getting too close to police work, too close to murder. Getting caught up in it somehow. I don't know if that's what happened to you . . ."

A door at the back of the hall opened. In stepped Eugene Green. He stood, unobtrusive, still, quiet, just inside the door, while Julian continued.

"What I do know is, you killed Sarah Langley, killed Wayne Hill, and when I got too close to the truth, tried to kill me too."

No one moved.

No one spoke.

No clinking of glass.

Not a breath.

Silence. The silence of the frozen North. The still, awkward, momentarily serene silence of the truth.

The first sound was sobbing,

then a wailing. . . .

Estelle, shoulders heaving, quickly hysterical. "Oh God . . . Oh God . . ."

The doors at the back of the hall opened. A handful of uniformed troopers stepped into the assembly hall. Chief Richards gestured to them from the side of the stage, not to take any action, to stay put.

Winston Edwards sat—still immobile, still impassive.

"This has been a remarkable internship, Winston," said Julian brightly. "I've really learned a lot."

She stepped back from the microphone, as Chief Richards stepped up to it. "Winston Edwards, you're under arrest for the murder of Sarah Langley. Of Wayne Hill. And the attempted murder of Julian Palmer."

He motioned the troopers in.

They moved around the tables toward Edwards. One took each of Edwards' arms.

They stood him up.

Estelle wailed.

The Great Bear stumbled a little on rising.

The wailing intensified. Still the only sound.

Edwards found his footing. Remained silent, eyes ahead, staring, unblinking, as he was escorted from the hall.

FORTY-THREE

Julian Palmer sat in Winston Edwards' ancient leather desk chair, regarding the high piles on the desk.

Chief Richards sat across from her, in the chair Julian had always occupied.

Julian scanned the piles of documents, then frowned suddenly, and took from the top of a lower pile a single sheet of paper.

Her resumé.

She smirked. Handed it to Richards.

"One thing I can't understand," said Richards. "If you're trying to cover up a murder, why hire an intern? Why risk it? I mean, another pair of eyes . . ."

"I understand it perfectly," said Julian, leaning back in the ancient leather chair, about to deliver her wisdom, not unaware of how the leaning-back motion and the delivered wisdom echoed with that of her former boss. "See, it can't be a Perfect Crime unless someone *knows* it's perfect." She leaned back, looked out the plate-glass window, examined the cornice of the Rhine Brothers roof across the street. "Winston Edwards needed a witness. A witness to his genius. Odd, isn't it, that for him, the Perfect Crime required a witness?"

A witness.

What Green had said he was.

Turned out he wasn't.

But by events he'd set in motion, a witness had been created. Julian had become the eyes, the ears, that Green had desperately longed to be. And while Green wasn't psychic, he had indeed turned out to be prophetic.

There was a knock at the office door. Richards was tall enough to reach back and open it a crack, to see who it was. He turned and looked at Julian. "Someone here to see you, Miss Palmer," he said, secretarially, amused.

Eugene Green entered the office.

He stood awkwardly, uncomfortably, unsure of himself.

"So," said Julian warmly.

"So," said Green, tentatively.

An awkward pause.

"What are you going to do now?" she asked him.

"Wait for the trial, I guess. Go back to Dr. Tibor in the meantime. I guess." A shrug. A listlessness. A lostness.

"I know how much you loved her, Eugene," Julian said quietly.

"How much we both did, apparently," answered Eugene, cynically. He looked down, seemed to examine his shoes. "My life. It's over," he said.

"Your life. It's beginning again," said Julian firmly, suddenly.

So suddenly, so firmly and forcefully, that Green looked at her with alarm.

"See you at the trial, Eugene Green."

"Yeah," he said, still looking at her. "See ya."

Green turned, left.

Richards took it as his cue. He rose laboriously from the chair.

"Guess I'll see you there too, Miss Palmer."

"See you at the trial, Chief Richards."

He smiled, turned, left.

Julian sat alone in Winston Edwards' office.

She leaned back again in the ancient chair.

And only then, remembered.

She opened the top drawer of Edwards' desk.

Took out the set of keys.

Turned, opened the file drawer behind her.

Reached in.

Pulled out the blue scarf.

Dropped it on the desktop.

White shoes. Blue scarf. Jade necklace.

A parody of clues.

But nevertheless, the clues.

She looked up at the far wall of the office, at the glass partition, where the gruesome eight-by-ten and sixteen-by-twenty glossies had hung.

"Sarah Langley. . . . A person. A life."

She could still hear him say it. Could still see his eyes narrow with significance, convey that look of profound human understanding. What part of the sentiment had he truly meant? What part had he concocted merely to convince her—with laconic efficiency—of his moral fiber, his unwavering resolve to find Sarah's killer?

A waitress. Alone in the world. Attracted in some powerful way to a man old enough to be her father, and magnetic enough, compelling enough, to be something more.

She felt Sarah suddenly. Felt her fully. Felt her as she never had before. Felt their souls touch across a fluttering, thin divide.

Maybe this was what it would mean to be a

woman in police work. To be closer to the victims somehow. To be forever with them.

What it would mean . . . Julian smiled, realizing what was implicit: that she already had made the decision, the commitment, somewhere within her, to continue as a woman in police work.

What could she do for Sarah Langley? How could she make the world's amends?

And for once, something was clear.

Out of complexity, simplicity.

What could she do? Simple:

She could live.

Fully.

Decisively.

Radiantly.

Julian Palmer. A person. A life.

She got up from the ancient leather chair. Took one last look around the office.

"See you at the trial, Winston Edwards."

She had learned enormously.

Had changed, had grown.

In that sense only, she thought ruefully, it had indeed been the Perfect Crime.

She walked out of the office of Winston Edwards, closing the door firmly behind her.

TURN THE PAGE FOR A LOOK AHEAD TO

THE HEAT OF LIES

ONE

"AHHH!" *Jesus! Sonavofuckingbitch!*

Lieutenant Palmer had just turned back from the big picture window of the cramped office six floors above Police Plaza, to hang up the phone after making yet another patiently irate call to Office Services checking on furniture ordered eight months ago, and there—seated silently in the wooden folding chair across the Lieutenant's crowded desk—was the first murderer Palmer had ever sent to prison.

Instinctively, the Lieutenant crossed her arms over her blouse to cover her breasts.

Her pulse surged. Her entire physiology sounded a well-orchestrated general alarm. Heart jumped, endorphins released, mouth went dry, stomach muscles clenched, in a fight-or-flight symphony of physical response. Memory came flooding back on a river of nausea. Five years, three promotions, twenty-four more murders and twenty-two murder convictions, had not, it appeared, sufficiently intervened.

Sonavofuckingbitch, she thought. But she wouldn't say it. Wouldn't give him the satisfaction.

In a reassuring instant, she saw that Mendoza and Ng were in a state of high alert at their desks just outside her office, looking warily and protectively and not least of all curiously in through her open door. It calmed her somewhat. She felt herself relax a degree.

She regarded the huge man cautiously, tensely, like eyeing a still-armed bomb. But now that she'd recovered from the shock of knowing him immediately, she saw that he was in fact almost unrecognizable. In the intervening five years, he'd aged unimaginably. His body, whose epic size had once projected immense power, now projected simply immensity—sloppy, uncooperative, defeated mass, rolling over the edges of the folding chair.

"How'd you get in here?"

"Flashed a badge," he said. Adding, "Old one."

His hair had gone fright white, thinned from a proud mane to a strandy wispiness. The furrowed facial lines that once evoked character and experience had finally overwhelmed his features, becoming simply wrinkles, like any old man's. His skin was ashen, chalky, like a patient's.

Beneath the wrinkles, though, his eyes still harbored some semblance of that nasty, restless alertness—now even more startling, in contrast to the thick, loose, epidermal folds surrounding them. Rhinoceros eyes—steady, unblinking, uncaring, brute.

Apart from the eyes, he looked close to death.

Close, she thought, but no cigar.

She appraised him silently for another long moment, before asking—carefully measuring her tone to be flat, without judgement or affront, like a disinterested clerk gathering information for a form—"What are you doing here?"

The unblinking eyes wandered over the unadorned green institutional walls of the tiny room aimlessly. He shrugged noncommitally.

She asked again—evenly, identically—as if he hadn't heard her the first time, which, given his startling aged appearance, he genuinely might not have—"What are you doing here?"

Another shrug.

She noted the rumpled white shirt beneath the open trenchcoat. Its collar, its cuffs, no longer crisply starched. "Wife finally threw you out, didn't she?" observed Lieutenant Palmer.

The man's eyebrows went up briefly, momentarily impressed with her deduction, then down again, sullenly confirming that it was correct.

She noticed the dirt ingrained on his shirt cuffs. Noticed that his left shoe heel was turned somewhat, askew beneath the rest of his shoe.

"Defense like that'll cost you, won't it?" she speculated further.

His lack of response was acknowledgement enough.

Whatever nestegg he'd managed to hide from the forensic accountants, whatever on-the-take money he'd augmented it with, had apparently gone significantly toward the fees of the famously brilliant and famously expensive attorney, one Lawrence Cooperman, Esq.

And it had been an exceedingly long defense, after all, longer than anyone could have predicted. Maybe he'd even had something on Cooperman as well—she had a nagging sense there was more to know about Cooperman's advocacy. His defense might have expended all his capital—the conventional green sort, and his deep hoard of black currency as well. Regardless, it had done its job.

Ladies and gentlemen, it is the word of one woman, a police officer at the outset of her career, against the word of another police officer, in the twilight of his. That's the cold truth of it. So do you believe the word of police officers, or don't you? Do they tell the truth, or are they liars?

Cooperman's cynical, sneering disregard for the proceedings in general. Inviting the jury to share that cynicism; cozying up to them.

Now if you think police officers are generally liars, then this little sampling would suggest you're onto something. And if you think they generally tell the truth, then based on this little sampling at least, you'd have to rethink that, wouldn't you?

The adeptness of the lawyer's delivery; coupled with the impression, the force, of slow, seamless, confident logic. She still heard it. It still pained her . . .

She held now to her careful monotone. Continued to speak, firm, clear, her trademark gentle interrogative, a mere notch above a whisper.

"What're you going to do?"

He shrugged.

What happened to that young waitress out there in the snow, let's face it, we're never going to know. We have two conflicting versions of events, and we'll simply never know which version matches the truth, if either . . .

"Where you gonna go?"

He shrugged again.

The alleged murder weapon was never found. Lost in an evidential mix-up in the small upstate police department that, it's been implied, he somehow controlled. I can only tell you that unfortu-

nately and statistically, crucial evidence is lost and misplaced all the time, in departments of all sizes, everywhere . . .

She'd put him in prison five years ago, and naturally had gotten used to picturing him there. But it had proved particularly onerous for the State to find an acceptable venue for his trial, given his local reputation, and the sparseness of options in that sparely populated upstate New York county. As a result, he'd waited in prison a long time. Months had stretched to years. Legal technicalities and issues and delays had presented themselves aboundingly. Until at last, the trial had begun.

She's a poised, beautiful young woman. He's a powerful, hated, difficult man. Right there, that makes me doubt, makes me suspect, the easy version of events, the version the prosecutors are trying to serve up; right there, that makes me listen again to the less palatable version . . .

Even then, there were further technicalities; another change of venue, witness-tampering and jury-tampering accusations and counter-accusations, false starts and full stops.

And the trial itself. Cameras banned. Access limited. Conducted during a brutal February of a brutal winter at the Canadian border. The venue inaccessible. A judge who would not allow a circus. This is no Heisman trophy winner, the bald hawk-nosed judge had smirked. The public has a right to know, yes, but not a right to watch. The reporters, and thus the public, could barely follow it. Soon lost interest in the legal tangle. Precisely what Lawrence Cooperman no doubt intended.

No weapon. No witnesses. Just she said he said. I'm frankly surprised that the State chose to proceed on such meager evidential grounds. Political pressure? Pressure exerted by vocal friends of the young officer? By well-placed enemies of the famously difficult defendant? Don't discount it. It would at least explain why we're all here . . .

And under the law, it had had to be divided, into distinct and separate proceedings. Further diluting, further dulling, the incidents' sum of impact. The trial itself had solely concerned the murder of the waitress. In a few hours one morning, Julian delivered her testimony; her testimony was challenged; and that was the extent of her role and her presence.

The State chose not to proceed at all in the matter of the suspected murder of psychic Wayne Hill. No evidence. No body. And a long and documented history of erratic behavior, sudden self-exiles, even periodic disappearances, on the part of the purported decedent. There was nothing but Julian's accusation: that Hill had been killed to cover up the waitress' murder. But she soon saw how that accusation—with no evidence behind it—undercut her credibility, even in the eyes of the prosecutors.

As for the accused's attempt on the life of Julian Palmer? Evidence nonexistent. Details extremely vague. Night. A blizzard. White-out conditions. Zero visibility. And because it was a matter between police officers, servants of the State, the State interceded on its own behalf. The career of a promising young police officer, in the State's view, should not be jeopardized; nor should the reputation of an acclaimed senior officer be needlessly compromised. In the absence of physical evidence, the State concluded, the matter should be adjudicated privately. Counsellors to both parties—each feeling an advantage to themselves—unhesitatingly agreed. And so it became a closed hearing. An internal affair, thick with procedure, rich with technicality. Documents. Closed-door presentations. Arbitration and mediation panels. A police matter. And a muddling, obfuscatory mess.

Both of their versions are in some sense convincing, because we are here, after all, considering them each carefully. Then again, neither is convincing enough. Because neither version, I'll wager right now, has flatly convinced any of you.

It was all long ago now. Another place. Another lifetime. A handful of senior officials here knew of the events, and that was it.

In the intervening years, she'd become used to the world's greys. To its imperfections, to its drift and sway, the certainty of its uncertainty. She still didn't accept it. But she did now at least expect it.

You can't convict. Even if you think he did it, even if you feel somehow certain of that, you can't convict. Much as you might want to. Much as you might hate him. Because you haven't got one piece of credible reliable evidence with which to do it.

"You're a murderer," she said to him now. Reminding him of the fact—as quietly, as flatly, as matter of factly—as she had said everything else.

And only now did he finally turn his attention, his famous gaze, directly at her. And only now did he speak, the first words in that crusty, deep-mean voice she had not heard in five years. "But not a convicted murderer," he said as quietly back.

And suddenly, the smile. Brazen and infuriating, unregenerate and unchanged . . .

She pushed the intercom button.

Mendoza and Ng were flanking the strange immense figure before she even had to say their names. But they wore looks of confusion as loud as orange raid jackets.

"Detective Mendoza, Detective Ng, meet Winston the Bear Edwards. Former Chief of Police of

Canaanville, NY., who I interned with five years ago . . ."

Ng smiled broadly, relieved, before the rest of her introduction robbed him of his congeniality . . .

"He stabbed a waitress forty-six times. Killed a man to try to cover it up. And when I went tumbling over a ledge, he thought he killed me too . . ." She could see the shock register on their faces. Big Ng looking incredulously at the old broken form seated in the chair, while the wiry, muscle-y Mendoza looked as incredulously directly at her. They knew she didn't lie. She didn't fool around. That's why they were having such a hard time with it.

"And not knowing where to go, he's come to see us. Like all the other flotsam and jetsam that washes up here. He doesn't know what he's doing here. Or he's not saying."

Now she was standing by the ancient crooked coat tree, lifting her own black trenchcoat off and swirling it onto her shoulders, having first, as always, strapped the service revolver on—an accessory, a necessity, like a handbag or wallet or keys.

"I want him watched, day and night," she told them. "I want a man tailing him everywhere. I want a man stationed in the hall of his fleabag hotel. I want someone beside him when he goes through restaurant trash. When he drinks rotgut, I want someone to know the brand. When he sleeps in the gutter, I want someone to watch him snore. He says he doesn't know what he's doing here. But we're going to. Every moment. Every move."

The short tirade had loosed her feelings, she discovered. They'd snuck out, leaked beneath the cold steel door of her professionalism, and now were gathering into a torrent she felt less and less control over . . .

She was as surprised as anyone to suddenly find the black muzzle of her service revolver sunk deep into Winston Edwards' mouth; before she could even process who exactly had done such a thing; before Mendoza and Ng could even respond with wide-eyed wordless shock.

Only Edwards seemed not to react. Looking up at her with big sleepy eyes behind the rhinocerative, pale, unhealthy folds.

You don't care, do you?, she thought. A valuable perception . . . store it away . . .

Of course, she was now indicating how deeply *she* cared.

She was showing him—once again—the depth of her feeling for him.

She pulled the muzzle from his mouth.

And was nearly as surprised as before to find the same muzzle now running high along his gums, making each tooth appear individually, sorrowfully, in a broken, ulcerative, yellowed periodontal parade. Livestock, examined meanly.

"He's a free man now," Julian said with mock gospel exuberance. "He can do whatever he wants."

Now she pressed the revolver muzzle hard just below his right eye, gathering up and pulling down the loose skin beneath the eye with it, opening the eye brutally, comically wide.

She put her own eye just above his brutally opened one, made a show of peering in, as if to see for herself the precise shape of the evil inside. A gemologist, appraising a strange brown stone in its crusted, folded setting.

She pressed the gun muzzle beneath his left eye now, pulled down, the folds of skin following helplessly obedient, a wake of stretched flesh. She made the same optometric inspection.

Mendoza shifted his feet uncomfortably. She heard Ng's breath come short and loud and nervous. Edwards never moved.

Now she pushed the muzzle against his right nostril. Lifted the outer edge meanly. Distorting the entire nose harshly for a long, held moment.

Lifted the right nostril identically.

Mendoza, Ng stood, transfixed.

She pulled the gun muzzle away, holstered it mechanically.

Regarded Edwards once more in that rickety folding chair.

Then reared her foot back and with all her gathered fury kicked the left-front leg of the wooden chair. The same left-front leg she'd seen threatening to give way on previous occupants for months now—eager clerks, nervous sergeants, Ng and Mendoza themselves.

The chair leg snapped crisply and cooperatively, and the two-hundred-eighty pounds of Winston the Bear Edwards puddled onto the floor sideways, gracelessly on top of it, aided in speed and awkwardness by the immensity and unpreparedness of the weight . . .

Beyond the sound of the broken wooden chair hitting the wooden floor, though, there was no accompanying sound from Winston Edwards. No involuntary huhn, no raging curse, no strangled syllable of surprise, nothing. Only a studied, respectful, obedient silence. Maybe stoic and challenging. Maybe mocking. Maybe just silent stunned surprise.

Slowly, the huge form splayed face down on the floor managed to turn its immense ursine head slightly toward her, to crane its neck just enough to present a brown pupil to her, peering out cautiously from behind the curtainous folds of skin.

She stood over the brown pupil purposefully, to fill its vision with the bottom of her trenchcoat, to momentarily overwhelm it with her presence.

"Welcome to the big city," she said.

She adjusted the holster, buttoned her trench-coat over it, clutched her handbag. "*My* city," she added. A perhaps unnecessary amplification.

She looked up at Mendoza and Ng. "I'm due at a deposition across town," she told them.

She headed briskly out the open office door.

It was frankly all she could think to do.

And with any luck, it would at least speed that furniture along.